let *go*

DARCY BURKE

For my good friend Elisabeth Naughton, who would not let up about this series! I hope it's everything you dreamed it to be.

Let Go

Breaking free from her structured life, Chloe English quits her high-powered job and moves across the country to work as an art teacher. The simple life is all she hoped it would be until her house burns down, leaving her homeless. When a handsome firefighter swoops in to save the day, she can't believe her luck. He's laid-back and unassuming, everything she's looking for in a man—or so he seems. It turns out he's as ambitious as her ex, comes with a family who could be more stifling than hers, and harbors dark secrets he may never be able to share.

Orphaned as a teenager, Derek Sumner has found a place in his best friend's family. However, the love and support of his surrogate parents and siblings can't erase the grief and loss he struggles every Christmas to banish. But this year he meets the fun and sexy Chloe, whose optimism and sense of joy are incredibly contagious. Can she help him face his bleak past so they can forge a happy future?

Don't miss the rest of the ***Ribbon Ridge*** series!

Do you want to hear all the latest about me and my books? Sign up at <u>Reader Club newsletter</u> for members-only bonus content, insider scoop, my exciting (ha!) diary (with cat pictures usually), as well as contests and giveaways!

Care to share your love for my books with like-minded readers? Want to hang with me and see pictures of my cats (who doesn't!)? Join my exclusive Facebook group, Darcy's Duchesses.

Chapter One

Ribbon Ridge, Oregon, December

Chloe English shivered against the cold wind sweeping down the street as she departed the door of the Arch and Vine brewpub, but her step was light and her heart warm. It was just three weeks to Christmas and though she was in a new town and had no friends or family nearby, she was optimistic that she'd made the right choice in moving across the country.

And to prove herself correct, she'd just landed a job as the Arch and Vine's newest server. Combined with what she'd earn from her part-time teaching job that was due to start in January, the wages would ensure she could live comfortably, if not extravagantly. Not that she needed to live extravagantly—that was her mother's dream, not hers.

Happiness and hope buoyed her gait as she made her way to her car down the block. A soft mist—even the rain here was pretty—began to fall as she climbed into her trusty Honda Civic and fired up the engine.

The giddy feeling in her chest remained during the fifteen-minute drive to her little rental house in the countryside near the edge of Ribbon Ridge. It was the most remote place she'd ever lived, but it was all she could afford. Plus, she liked the quaint arched doorways and old-fashioned built-ins, though she had to admit she was still learning to appreciate the lack of a dishwasher.

She bobbed her head to silly songs on the radio sung by pink-haired pop stars and cute British boy bands and marveled at how well things had turned out. Her mother would hate that. She was so waiting for Chloe to pack up and come home before Christmas and admit she'd been wrong to uproot herself. Fat chance of that happening.

The song, however, died from Chloe's lips as she saw orange flames slithering into the dark night sky. There were just two houses along the narrow lane—hers and another one a quarter mile down the road.

The closer Chloe got, the colder she felt. Her house was on fire. Really, really on fire. She parked across the street from the fire truck and jumped out of her car.

"Oh, Chloe!" Mrs. Boatwright, her sole neighbor, called, striding quickly toward Chloe. Her gray hair was clipped up, and she wore a light blue raincoat and a pair of bright orange Crocs with fuzzy inserts. "I didn't know how to reach you, sorry. I had to call 911."

"I'm glad you did." Chloe wanted to ask what Mrs. Boatwright had done with her cell phone number, which she'd given her just the other day when they'd met, but recalled the woman's rather messy house and decided it was probably lost amidst all of the magazines, junk mail, and other clutter. "Do you know when the fire started?" Chloe's gaze fixated on the orange-yellow flames licking up the front of the little house. The fire had engulfed the entire left side of the structure, leaving the garage on the right mostly untouched—so far.

She wished she hadn't gotten so far with her unpacking. If she hadn't, some of her clothes and other things would still be in the garage and might have been salvaged. She'd even hung most of her pictures and artwork, save about four canvases she hadn't gotten to yet.

Mrs. Boatwright patted Chloe's shoulder. "I noticed the flames maybe an hour ago. Took the engine almost twenty minutes to get here."

Chloe was surprised they'd arrived so quickly, given the location of the house and the fact that the fire station was on the opposite side of town.

Just then, a slim, middle-aged man approached them. "Are you Miss English?" he asked.

Chloe nodded, a lump forming in her throat at the sympathy in his tone. "I am."

His friendly face was weathered, as if he'd fought a hundred fires. "I'm Hank Johnson, the fire chief. Mrs. Boatwright said you lived alone. So there's no one else inside? Any pets?"

Chloe shook her head. "No, just me. What happened?"

His forehead crinkled and he took her hand between his large, gloved palms. "Let us put the flames out and then we'll figure out what happened, okay?" He gave her an encouraging look—it wasn't a smile, but it was warm and gave Chloe a modicum of comfort.

Mrs. Boatwright had kept her hand on Chloe's shoulder and resumed patting it for a moment. "I'm glad you weren't home."

"Me too. But maybe . . ." If she'd been there she could've stopped it before the fire had progressed.

Mrs. Boatwright removed her hand and crossed her arms as she watched the firefighters battle the flames. "You can stay with me, if you like. I don't have a spare room, but I have a couch. I'll just kick the dogs off it."

Her four very large dogs who took up what space was available in Mrs. Boatwright's small house that was chock full of stuff. "I appreciate the offer, Mrs. Boatwright, and if I need a place to stay, you'll be the first person I call." Before she resorted to that, she'd try one of the bed-and-breakfasts in town. She didn't have a ton of savings, but she had plenty of room on her credit cards—not that she wanted to max anything out. Right now, though, things seemed bleak enough that it might come to that. Where was she going to go?

Her focus returned to the house and the men working to put out the fire. Watching it burn, she felt like the world was falling away, like everything she'd planned and dreamed by coming here on her own was disappearing before her very eyes. Tears of sadness and frustration trailed down her cheeks, mixing with the rain, which had started falling harder. It wasn't fair! She'd worked so hard to move here, to start over. It was like Fate was telling her to go home.

She wouldn't go. Home was wherever she chose it to be, and damn it, she chose here. She wiped her cheeks and stuck out her chin. She chose Ribbon Ridge.

"Hey! There's a cat here!" A tall firefighter rushed around the house, coming from the back. He cradled a tiny bundle in the crook of his arm as he ran to Chloe. "Is this your kitten?"

Chloe's gaze landed on the tiny ball of wet, gray fur nestled against his wet, soot-smeared coat. Her heart seized. "Where did you find that? Is it . . . ?" She couldn't bring herself to say "dead."

He looked down at the kitten. "She's breathing. I think she'll be fine. I found her near the back porch." He turned the full focus of his dark-as-midnight eyes on Chloe. "But she's not yours?"

Chloe shook her head.

"I think there might be something wrong with her eyes, there's some leakage. Can you hold on to her for now?" He held the animal toward Chloe. "I need to get back."

"Of course." Chloe brought the kitten to her chest and snuggled it inside her coat for warmth. The poor thing was ice-cold and sopping wet.

The firefighter returned to battling the flames and after another quarter hour or so, Chloe finally retreated to the relative warmth and dryness of her car. Inside, she grabbed her favorite hoodie, which was in the backseat from a few days ago, and wrapped the kitten up in it. She kept the bundle on her lap, rotating the jacket to a new dry spot when it got too damp against the kitten, and stroked the tiny animal while she watched her house burn.

Hours later, the fire was finally out. All that remained of her cute, little house was a roofless, charred shell. What hadn't been destroyed by the flames was surely toast from the water. *Toast?!*

With the fire extinguished, the firefighters seemed to move into clean-up mode. The fire chief came over and took Chloe's statement as well as her contact information. He said he'd be in touch tomorrow morning. He'd tried to reach her landlord, but hadn't been able to get hold of him.

"He's in Mexico for the holidays," Chloe said, numbly.

After the chief returned to the house and his crew, the tall firefighter approached her car. Chloe got out to meet him.

"You okay?" he asked, his gaze searching for the kitten and settling on it snuggled in the front passenger seat.

"I'm fine," she said, not meaning it in the slightest.

"You're not fine. Your house just burned down." He flinched as he realized he'd not only stated the obvious, but that he'd bluntly reminded her of the awfulness of her situation.

"Yeah, I get that," she said, though she wasn't angry at him for saying it. She was angry at life.

"Sorry." And by the concern in his dark eyes, she knew

he meant it sincerely. "He nodded toward the kitten. "What are you going to do about her?"

"Keep her." She glanced at the kitten curled up in her hoodie, as if she were Chloe's sole remaining anchor. And maybe she was. "Unless someone claims her." *God, please let no one claim her.* Chloe might really lose it then, and she was only barely keeping herself together.

The firefighter's gaze flicked toward the kitten. "Maybe I want her."

Chloe opened her mouth to tell him off, but belatedly heard the slight teasing note in his voice. He was trying to lighten a horrific mood, and on some level she appreciated that, though it was damned hard to show it. "Sorry, Ashley is spoken for."

"Ashley?"

Chloe blinked at him. "She's gray."

He laughed, and the sound was deep and rich and pleasant. It soothed her frazzled nerves and gave her at least a moment's solace. "Fair enough. You gave a statement to the chief, right? You didn't have a Christmas tree, did you?"

"Not yet."

He nodded. "It would've been the easy culprit, but something else caused the fire, then. No appliances left on? A curling iron or something? No candles burning?" He held up his hand. "Never mind, I'm sure the chief already went over this with you. I'm so sorry this happened. We'll figure it out."

She deeply appreciated his care and concern, but tears were clogging her throat and she couldn't speak.

As if sensing her distress, he laid his hand on her shoulder. "You'll get through this. Do you have family you can call?" He looked around as if just noticing she was all alone. And man, was she *alone.* If she called her parents now, they'd insist she jump on the first plane back to Pittsburgh and abandon her dream of a new life.

But she refused to run home now. It would take a lot more than a fire to end her plans. "I don't. I only moved here about ten days ago. I have a room at a bed-and-breakfast in town—the Blackberry Inn."

He tipped his hat back and frowned. "I don't think you can take Ashley there. If you like, I can take her. Temporarily," he rushed to add. "I promise I'll give her back."

She eyed him warily, but in the end she wanted to trust him—needed to in order to survive this horrible night. "Thank you, I'd appreciate that." She turned and carefully lifted the kitten, still wrapped in her hoodie, from the car and handed her to the firefighter. "She seems to have warmed up, but I'm sure she could use some food. And I think you're right that there's something wrong with her eyes."

He took the kitten from her and looked at the tiny gray face. "I know the vet in town. I'll have him take a look at her first thing in the morning."

Chloe could hardly believe his generosity. Tears threatened again, but she fought them back. "Thank you. I can't even tell you how much I appreciate your kindness."

"It's my duty. And my pleasure." He smiled, and for the first time in hours, Chloe had an urge to smile back. But she didn't. Couldn't. Not yet. "Why don't you head to the Blackberry?" he said. "The chief will be in touch with you tomorrow. And I'll get your number from him so I can return your cat."

She nodded, suddenly weary to the bone. "Thank you. Again."

He cuddled Ashley, and Chloe was touched by the juxtaposition of the tiny ball of fur snuggled against a broad-shouldered, six-foot-two man—with a heart-stoppingly handsome face. "Get some sleep. Tomorrow will be better."

It had to be, right?

He reached over and held her car door while she climbed inside. With a final, grateful look in his direction, she started her car and turned it around before driving down the lane, careful to avert her eyes from the remains of her home.

The drive to town seemed to take forever, but maybe that was due to her exhaustion. It was practically the middle of the night, after all. Or maybe it was due to the fact that she was driving abnormally slowly. It was as if she was incapable of moving forward.

Frustrated with herself for succumbing to self-pity, she shook her shoulders and applied her foot to the gas pedal.

She was going to get through this. It would take a lot more than a fire to get Chloe English down.

She pulled over when she got into town to look up the address of the Blackberry Inn. It was on Copper Lane, but she wasn't exactly sure where that was. She pulled up the navigation system and realized it was a couple miles out of town, thankfully not in the direction she'd just come from. Armed with directions courtesy of Mapquest, she headed toward the inn, her body anxious for a bed and maybe a warm bath. She smelled like smoke, which wasn't a great aroma, particularly when it reminded you that you'd just lost most of what you owned. At least her summer clothes were still in Pittsburgh.

Ten minutes later, she drove past a painted sign that read BLACKBERRY INN and pulled into a gravel lane. A large, '8os-style house came into view. Not exactly the quaint country bed-and-breakfast she had in mind. It was also completely dark, save for the exterior lights flooding the driveway.

She parked the car, grabbed her purse—because it was the only thing she had—got out, and made her way to the front door. She knocked softly, not wanting to wake any of the guests since it was past 2 A.M. When no one came, she knocked harder. Still nothing. A furtive search for a doorbell revealed nothing. After another minute or two of knocking and no response, Chloe pulled out her phone and dialed the inn's number. After three rings, the voicemail picked up. No, she didn't want to leave a message about making a reservation. She wanted to *claim* her reservation.

She didn't know what to do—simple decision-making seemed quite beyond her at this point. Pound on the door and scream to wake the dead? Or just go somewhere else? But where? She supposed she could drive to the next town —a good twenty-five minutes at least—and see if the hotel there had a vacancy. After waffling another minute, she decided she couldn't bring herself to make a scene. The other guests didn't deserve to have their sleep interrupted because the innkeeper had forgotten about her.

As she made her way back to the car, she finally heard the door open. She swung around expectantly.

"What is it?" the man asked, his voice thick with sleep.

Chloe retraced her steps to the door, relieved she didn't have to leave after all. "I have a reservation."

"At two o'clock in the morning?" He sounded quite cranky, not that Chloe blamed him. She *had* woken him up in the middle of the night. But then, he *was* running a business. "I don't have any rooms available."

"What?" Chloe didn't bother hiding her frustration. "I called earlier tonight and was told you had a room. I gave you my credit card number."

"Me? No. We only have two rooms and they're booked all week. Must've been someplace else."

Oh, God. What had she done? She'd been so upset. Flustered. But she couldn't go and stay with Mrs. Boatwright. She'd just as soon sleep in her car.

"You all right?" he asked, staring at her face.

Chloe realized tears had started leaking down her cheeks. "Yes." Why lie? "No. My house just burned down and I don't have anywhere to go." The tears threatened to come in earnest and she didn't want to break down in front of this stranger. "Do you know where I can go?"

He opened the door a little wider. "Here. I have a couch, at least, in the common room downstairs. You can sleep there." He gestured for her to come in and moved aside as she did so.

"Thank you." She used the back of her hand to dry her cheeks and sniffed.

He moved through the entry, which was only lit by the exterior light shining through a window over the door, and into a sunken living area. He turned on a lamp next to a large sofa that looked comfortable and inviting. At last, the tension left her shoulders.

He gestured toward an end table. "There are some tissues there. I'll get you a pillow and some blankets."

"I can't thank you enough for your hospitality. I have no idea who I called earlier, but I appreciate you coming to the rescue." Right along with the fireman who had saved the cat.

"We take care of people here in Ribbon Ridge. I'll be right back." He turned and disappeared up the stairs into a lit hallway above.

Chloe blew her nose and decided things could be much worse. She'd only lost things in the fire. Replaceable, mostly meaningless things. Okay, she couldn't replace her artwork, her lucky paintbrush, or her favorite blanket she'd had all through college, but she could start over. Wasn't that why'd she'd come here in the first place?

Yes, this could be a disaster, or it could be a completely new start. And judging by the kindness of strangers in Ribbon Ridge, she could do far worse.

The innkeeper came back and provided her with bedding as well as a towel. And a long floral nightgown that looked like something Chloe's grandmother might wear. "I thought you might need something to sleep in. There's a bathroom through there." He pointed toward a short hallway next to the stairs. "No shower, but you can clean up in the sink well enough. There's some extra toothbrushes and whatnot in the cabinet. My wife keeps the place pretty well stocked. Oh," he cringed slightly, "speaking of my wife, she'll start rattling around in the kitchen around 6:30. Sorry about that."

Chloe doubted she'd sleep anyway. "That's no problem at all. I'm just thankful for your hospitality."

After he'd gone back upstairs, Chloe peeled off her wet coat and hung it on a hook in the entryway and went straight to the bathroom. Once she'd washed her hair in the sink and erased as much of the smoky smell from her person as she could, she returned to the living room wearing the nightgown, for which she was immensely grateful. Then she made up the couch and climbed into "bed." She expected to lie awake until the sun rose, but instead fell into a deep sleep almost immediately.

And she dreamed of a tiny, gray kitten snuggled against a spectacularly gorgeous fireman, whose name she didn't even know.

Chapter Two

It was nearly 6 a.m. before Derek Sumner and the rest of the fire crew were done with Chloe English's house. Derek went to the fire chief's rig where Ashley was sleeping in the front seat. She was still snuggled in Chloe's hoodie, but had also been swaddled with one of Hank's spare shirts, which he kept in the back of the SUV. Everyone had taken turns checking on the animal.

"Sumner!" Hank came toward Derek. "Can I drop you and the cat at home? The other guys have got the engine." The extra tender truck had left hours ago.

"Actually, do you mind dropping me at the Archers'?" It was half the distance to Derek's loft in town, and Emily Archer would be happy to take care of Ashley while Derek got cleaned up and caught a few hours of sleep.

"Not at all."

Ten minutes later, Hank drove up the quarter-mile

drive leading to the Archer family home, a huge arts-and-crafts–style mansion. The drive was lit every hundred feet, and because it was Christmastime, the bulbs had been changed to alternating green and red. Though it was still dark, the lights on the house had shut off hours ago. If they'd been on, the glow would've lit up the countryside—it wasn't quite a Griswold Christmas, but it was close. Robert and Emily Archer loved the holidays. In fact, Derek had never known anyone who loved them more, and it was thanks to them that this time of year had finally begun to mean more than just painful memories.

He shook the past away as Hank pulled into the circular drive and dropped him at the base of the stone steps. Derek picked up Ashley, thanked Hank for the lift, and dragged his tired body up to the front terrace and massive entry.

He unlocked the door and let himself in.

Robert Archer rushed out of his office, which was just off the entry hall, coffee cup in hand. He'd always been an early riser. Tall and slim with thick gray hair that still boasted a few strands of dark brown here and there, he was fit and robust for sixty, which wasn't surprising given his passion for cycling. "Derek? What brings you here at this hour?" His gaze fell on Derek's outfit and he said, "There was an actual fire?"

Derek was one of sixteen volunteer firefighters in Ribbon Ridge, and in his five years of service they'd never had more than a burning pan on a stove or a backyard fire that had started to get out of line. "Yeah, a small house out on McMurtry Lane."

"Not Mrs. Boatwright's?" Robert knew everyone in Ribbon Ridge, and he certainly knew every bit of real estate. He owned probably 60 percent of it, and his family had founded the town over a hundred fifty years ago.

Derek shook his head. "The other one."

Rob wrinkled his nose beneath his reading glasses. "Vic Enders owns that place." Vic owned a bunch of properties in Ribbon Ridge and neighboring towns. He was notorious for being a slumlord, and Rob took pleasure in stealing properties out from under him before Vic could run them into the ground and take advantage of the tenants.

Derek was sorry Chloe had rented from the deadbeat. He hoped she didn't have trouble dealing with him, particularly since the evidence they'd found laid the blame for the fire cleanly at his feet. "Faulty wiring in the walls. Looks like he tried to upgrade the electric to meet code, but cut some corners."

Rob shook his head. "What a shame. I feel sorry for his tenants. They okay?"

"I think so. It's just a single woman. New to town."

Rob inclined his head toward the kitten in Derek's arms. "Is that her cat?"

Derek stroked the animal's soft fur. "Sort of. At least she is now."

"Who's here?" Emily Archer, the woman Derek considered his second mother and loved every bit as much as his first, came into the entryway. "Derek! Why are you standing there in your gear? You look exhausted. And what is that, a kitten?" She bustled toward him, her robe drawn tight over her petite frame. Before Derek could protest, she'd swept Ashley from his arms, not that he'd expected anything less. Emily's heart was a force of nature.

"Yes, we think it might have something wrong with its eyes. I wanted to take her in to see Sam this morning."

"I'll take care of it, dear." Emily petted the cat fondly as she looked up at Derek. "You look dead on your feet. Why don't you go on home?"

"Actually, I had Hank drop me off here so I could grab a shower and a nap before work."

"Work?" Rob shook his head. "Why would you go in to work today? Forget that."

Derek was the CFO of Archer Enterprises, so if the CEO told him he shouldn't go to work, who was he to argue? "Okay. But I'm filling in this afternoon at the pub. Mike's shorthanded."

"That's so nice of you." Emily smiled warmly at him. "You have such a generous heart. But go on, take your shower. I've got your cat."

"Not my cat, Chloe's."

Emily glanced at Rob as if he might have the answer. "Who's Chloe?"

Rob shrugged. "I'm guessing she's the tenant of the house that burned down tonight."

"Oh!" Emily's mouth dropped in horror. "That's awful! I should've realized there was an actual fire. You wouldn't be doing a training exercise in the middle of the night. How did you come to have Chloe's cat?"

"She's staying at the Blackberry Inn tonight. She's new to town, no family, no friends." He ached for her loss. "I offered to take care of Ashley."

Rob coughed to cover up a laugh. "The cat's name is *Ashley*?"

Derek smiled. It was hard to say for sure, but he thought Chloe was in possession of a great sense of humor. Why else would she name the kitten Ashley? "It seemed appropriate, given that I found it outside of a burning house. And she's gray."

"So she is," Emily murmured. "Well, I'll take care of Miss Ashley."

Derek had thought of something on the way over and now seemed like as good a time as any to ask. "Speaking of Chloe, do you think she could stay in the apartment over the garage until she finds a new place?"

"Of course!" Emily said quickly, then sucked in a breath. "But we have guests coming on the fifteenth."

Derek's brain froze for a moment. December 15 was the worst day on the calendar.

"Unfortunately, she'll need to be out by then," Emily continued, sounding regretful. "Unless she wants to stay in one of the kids' rooms." The Archers' house contained nine bedrooms—one for Rob and Emily and every one of their children, including Derek. "I'm sure at least one of them will be available. It's not like they all come home for the holidays, except for the Christmas party, and that's on

Saturday." The company Christmas party was the one time each year when all of their seven kids—plus Derek—would be in the same place, a fact that never failed to disappoint Emily.

"There's another option," Rob said slowly, fixing his gray gaze on Derek. "Have you decided whether you're going to sell your house?"

God, the fifteenth *and* his house in the same conversation? They were both things he tried to ignore. And unfortunately couldn't. He hadn't lived in the house since his mother had died ten years ago, but he also hadn't been able to sell it and sever the last tie to his youth. Rob's property management company rented it out, and for the most part Derek went out of his way to avoid it. However, it was currently vacant, and Rob had asked him last week if he was finally ready to sell.

"Not yet." But Derek knew the answer was no. He was just too tired to get into it right now.

"So rent it to this Chloe," Emily suggested, nuzzling the kitten to her chest. "The last renters had their own furniture, but we can refurnish it from the management company's storage unit."

Rob took a sip of coffee. "That's what I was thinking. I believe there are painters and carpet cleaners scheduled this week, so we'll have to see when it's available."

Derek supposed he could rent it to her, but for some reason, he was hesitant. Why? Because he was sort of hoping he would see her socially, and he wasn't sure he wanted to do that in his old house. So he was going to deprive her of a perfectly good place to live because he wanted to ask her out?

Selfish much?

"I'll talk to her about it." He was already hoping she would decline.

"Excellent." Emily brought the kitten up and looked into its face. "You sweet little thing. Let's get you some food. I think I have some chicken liver in the fridge. And maybe some milk?" She looked past Ashley to Derek. "Can I get you anything, dear?"

"No, thank you. I'm just going to get cleaned up." He nodded at Rob and walked past Emily, pausing to kiss her on the cheek and give Ashley a quick pat.

"Leave your clothes outside your room and I'll throw them in the washer while you sleep," Emily called after him, making him smile with her welcome mothering.

Derek moved from the entry into the oval-shaped hall and inhaled the pine scent of the twenty-foot-tall Christmas tree peeking from the corner of the great room on the opposite side of the hall. A not-quite-life-size sleigh sat in the center of the oval. It was currently empty, but at the party this weekend, attendees would fill it with gifts for underprivileged kids. It was, like so many things in the Archers' lives, tradition, and Derek loved it.

As he made his way down the north wing and then downstairs, he marveled at how much this house felt like home. Unlike the house he'd lived in with his mother for eight years. But that time in his life held too many unpleasant memories. They'd never gotten over his father's death, and then she'd gotten sick. Why the hell wasn't he selling the place?

Because it was all he had of her. Of the time when he'd had a family. Not that he didn't have a family now, the Archers, a cousin of his father's he'd met once who lived in Boston, and his mother's estranged father who lived in Hong Kong and hadn't seen Derek since he was a baby—but it wasn't the same.

Downstairs, he went directly to his bathroom and peeled off his smoke-saturated clothes and tossed them outside the door for Emily to launder. Though he still kept some things in his room, he doubted he had any pajamas. No matter. He might just fall asleep in the shower.

As he climbed into bed a short while later, he saw Chloe's strong, but feminine heart-shaped face framed with dark blond hair, her hazel eyes looking up at him with such a deep fortitude that he smiled to himself. She'd faced the tragedy of the fire with amazing poise and courage. No hysterics. No meltdown of any kind. He really hoped she was okay. Maybe he should've insisted she come here instead of the Blackberry Inn. Emily would've welcomed her and taken care of her, just like she was doing with Ashley.

But that would've been terribly forward. It was already going to be a bit awkward to offer her a place to stay. And maybe to live. Could he go through with that? Could he invite her to live in his house?

His stomach clenched and cold sweat beaded his forehead. He flipped over to his side and punched the pillow to fluff it up beneath his head. For years, Rob and Emily had been trying to convince him to move on. Maybe now was the time.

And really, it probably didn't matter. Chloe was just a woman he'd helped at a fire. She wasn't his girlfriend—hell, she wasn't even his friend. After he returned her cat, he might never even see her again, interact with her, save for the occasional head nod if they passed each other on the street.

That thought didn't make him feel better at all.

***

Chloe had slept a good four hours at the Blackberry Inn, and she'd woken up feeling as refreshed as one could feel when they'd just lost their house to a fire. Until she'd called her landlord in Mexico to ask for her deposit, the last month's rent she'd prepaid, and the rest of this month's rent back. Why should he keep her money when the fire had been entirely his fault? Amazingly, she'd gotten him on the phone, but he'd put her off, telling her they'd settle things when he got back in January, after he'd had a chance to review what had happened. She'd told him she didn't think that would work for her, and that she'd see what an attorney had to say. Backpedaling wildly, Vic had told her his accountant would be in touch soon. Ha! Chloe wasn't the kind of person to sit meekly by and be taken advantage of.

Then she'd called her insurance company and filed a

claim. Getting those wheels in motion had given her a small bit of satisfaction. After that, she'd tracked down the bed-and-breakfast she'd actually called the night before—the Blackbird, not the Blackberry. She'd explained what had happened and they'd graciously offered not to charge her for last night. However, while they'd booked her a room for tonight instead, they were full for the weekend, so Chloe had to find something else fast. Plus, she had yet to hear from the fireman, whose name she hadn't bothered to ask amidst last night's commotion, and recover her kitten. She wondered how Ashley was doing and whether she'd been to the vet.

First, though, she had to start her job at the Arch and Vine Pub.

She walked into the pub at 11:15, wearing exactly what she'd worn yesterday, which still smelled vaguely of smoke despite her applying a few coats of Febreze from the Blackberry Inn's bathroom. And stopped short when the firefighter from last night walked up to her.

At least she thought it was the guy from last night. He was dressed completely differently: black V-neck t-shirt that fit his muscular frame to a T, dark-wash jeans, and scuffed leather boots. She hadn't been able to make out the color of his hair because he'd been wearing his fire helmet, but now saw that it was as dark as his shirt. And his eyes— she hadn't been able to see their color last night either— Lord, they were gorgeous. Deep, dark blue, like cerulean mixed with midnight. If her art supplies hadn't burned up, she would've gone home and tried to recreate that color.

"Chloe!" he said, sounding as surprised to see her as she felt upon seeing him.

"Um, hi," she said, at a loss for his name.

As if reading her mind, he said, "Oh geez. I didn't actually introduce myself last night, did I? I'm Derek. Sumner." He held out his hand and she put her palm to his. A shock of warmth rushed up her arm and spread into her chest.

She withdrew her hand before she could become officially tongue-tied. "How's Ashley?" she managed, trying to ignore the sensations just shaking his hand had wrought.

He put his hands on his waist, accentuating the slim line of his hips. If their touch had affected him, she couldn't tell. "Actually, Emily—she's uh, a really good friend—just called a little bit ago to say Ashley is doing well. She had a viral infection in her eyes. After a course of antibiotic drops, she'll be seeing as well as you or I. Or better, I guess. Cats see better than humans, don't they?"

"In the dark, at least." Chloe fixated for a moment on this Emily person. His description of her stuck out for some reason. Friend or girlfriend? Oh, why did it even matter? She was in no position to flirt with or date some hot firefighter.

She noticed the short, off-white apron tied around his hips. "Wait, do you work here?"

He shrugged one shoulder. "From time to time. I said I'd help out today because Mike's shorthanded. But he left a note that he hired a new server. Is that you?"

"It is."

"Great," he said, smiling, but then quickly frowned. "No. You shouldn't work today. We'll manage. You should go . . . uh . . ."

His words trailed off as he realized what he'd been about to say. She surprised herself by smiling. "Home? Right. Wish I had one."

"Actually, I can help you there, at least temporarily if you're interested."

Her mind immediately leapt to staying with him. On his couch. Or wherever. *Pull yourself together, Chloe!* "What do you have in mind?" She hadn't meant for that to sound flirtatious, but thought it probably did. Oops.

"My friend—Emily—has a furnished apartment over her garage. You're welcome to stay there until the fifteenth. Maybe you can find another place by then?"

"Maybe." Though she doubted it. That was only ten days away, and she'd performed an exhaustive search of rentals in the area before moving there. The cheapest rent was in Ribbon Ridge, as opposed to the larger towns surrounding it, and the most affordable property—by a lot —had been the little house that had burned to the ground. Given what she knew now about the condition of its wiring and the behavior of her landlord, she understood why it had been affordable. "In the meantime, I'd love to take your . . . friend up on her offer."

"Great. You can move in today, if you like. Although, I suppose you don't have anything to really move in." He peered at her from between half-closed lids, appearing sheepish. "Sorry."

All this talk of where she was going to live and the reminder that she had no belongings—save the toothbrush and other necessities she'd picked up that morning—was threatening to kill her optimism, and she desperately needed to cling to it. She glanced around. "So, where do I start?"

"You can't possibly think of working today," he said, looking at her like she'd sprouted another head.

"I really want to. It'll keep my mind off things. I've done everything I can. Plus, I need the money more than ever. Just let me call the Blackbird and cancel my stay."

"The Blackbird? I thought you were at the Blackberry." His forehead crinkled in an adorably confused way.

"Funny story." She related her mistaken reservation shenanigans. He laughed, and she surprised herself again by laughing with him. Then he offered her one of their Archer Pubs t-shirts advertising Will Scarlett, their raspberry ale, to wear instead of her smoke-laden top. She went back to the break room, where she stashed her purse in a locker, hung up her coat, and found one of the t-shirts to change into.

When she returned to the dining room, she saw that the first patrons of the day, two middle-aged men, were sitting beneath the mural she'd admired the night before. It had been painted to look like windows facing out onto a medieval English street. The detail was amazing and incredibly lifelike. She paused a moment to look at it, hoping she possessed even a tenth of that talent.

"You like the mural?" Derek asked as Chloe

approached him at the bar, which was situated in the center of the pub.

"It's beautiful." She'd studied the trompe l'oeil—as best as she could from the bar—while sampling the beer last night after Mike had hired her.

"Rob's uncle painted it."

Chloe pulled her attention from the painting. "Rob?"

"Archer. He owns the pubs. And he's your new temporary landlord." Derek pulled a pint of the seasonal beer from one of the ten taps. "He and his wife, Emily."

Oh. Emily really was just a friend. Or an employer who was a friend? "And she's taking care of Ashley?"

Derek pulled a second pint. "Yeah, she's great. She'll mother you too, if you let her."

"Should I?"

He grinned at her. "Most definitely. Be right back." He took off to deliver the beer to the two men.

The door to the pub opened then and a fifty-something-year-old man with glasses and buzzed gray hair came in. He strode directly toward the bar, then stopped short when he saw Chloe standing behind it. "What're you doing behind my bar?"

"George, it's not your bar," Derek said, returning, but there was zero heat to his words. "This is our new server, Chloe. Chloe, this is George, our daytime bartender. He's a bit of an OF—that's old fart—so don't take him seriously."

"Show me some respect, young man. I was an officer in the United States Marine Corps!" He pushed past Derek and went to a corner of the bar, pulled an apron from beneath it, and tied it around his waist. "Where's your apron, Chloe? Hasn't Derek shown you a darned thing?"

Derek rolled his eyes, but the smile on his lips indicated this was a friendly ribbing between two men who'd likely spent a lot of time working together. "She just got here, and we have customers. I was about to tell her about the beer."

"Lucky I showed up." George's brown eyes twinkled behind wire-rimmed bifocals. "No one pulls a more perfect pint than I do. Let me show you."

George spent the next ten minutes telling her about all the varieties and showing her how to pull a pint with just the right amount of head. He was so into his tutorial and his delivery was so engaging that Chloe didn't bother telling him she'd learned all of this from Mike, the pub manager, the day before.

"Have you had any beer, then?" George asked.

"I tried them all." She'd sampled one or two sips of everything, and maybe a little more of a few of them.

George leaned against the bar. "Which one's your favorite?"

"I like the Nock." The winter seasonal was a dark stout with a smooth, chocolate finish.

"Good choice. Derek here's a Crossbow lad through and through."

Chloe had learned that Crossbow was their signature ale. "I liked that one too, but I'm a beer girl and I liked them all. In fact, it's one of the reasons I chose to move to

Oregon. Great microbreweries." She turned her gaze to Derek.

His lips spread in a toe-curling grin. "And ours is the best."

"So far, yes." And as she took in his movie-star good looks, she realized she wasn't just talking about the beer. She hoped he didn't realize that too. The last thing she needed was a workplace flirtation on top of everything else. This job was more important than ever.

The day flew by as Chloe worked to stay on her toes. She welcomed the busy atmosphere of the pub, and chatting with the customers took her mind almost completely off her woes. By quitting time, she was too bone-tired to care that she didn't have pajamas to sleep in. Though maybe she could swipe another shirt from the pub's stock.

Derek approached her as she wiped down a table. "You should go. Here," he handed her a slip of paper, "these are directions to the Archers'."

Crud, she'd forgotten to call and cancel her reservation at the Blackbird, and she didn't feel right about doing it this late in the day—it was past 7:00. "You know, I think I'm going to stay at the B and B tonight. I'm exhausted, it's close. Win-win."

"I could drive you to the Archers," he offered, "but I'm not quite ready to leave."

"It's okay." She smiled at him reassuringly as she tucked the paper into her pocket. "You've already done so much. But, I *am* taking another shirt. I need pajamas."

His gaze dipped down her body briefly, but she caught

it. Heat swirled in Chloe's belly. She'd opened herself up to any number of cheesy pickup lines with that comment. Strangely, she wanted to hear every single one of them from Derek Sumner's lips.

"Take whatever you like." *Such a gentleman.* Chloe liked him even more. "Mike won't mind. And Emily texted me a little while ago to report that Ashley is doing well, so you don't need to worry about her. Though, if I were you, I'd claim that cat A-S-A-P before you can't pry it away from Emily's motherly grip. And not because Emily won't let her go, but because Ashley won't want to leave."

Emily sounded delightful. Chloe could hardly believe she was taking care of a sick, stray kitten for a woman she'd never met, and she'd offered to let that woman—Chloe— live in her apartment. Everyone in Ribbon Ridge had been so wonderful, her landlord notwithstanding, but then she reasoned that he didn't actually live in Ribbon Ridge. Despite him and the fire, she just couldn't bring herself to regret moving here.

"I'll go over there first thing tomorrow." Right after she got a good night's sleep. God, she hoped she had one.

"How about I meet you there? Introduce you to Robert and Emily, help you settle in."

Since she didn't require "settling" of any kind, she wondered at his motive. Then decided she didn't care, that she'd take any excuse to hang out with him, her first real friend in Ribbon Ridge.

"Sure."

He smiled. "You a coffee or tea girl?"

"Either, really. Though I love the chais from that coffee drive-through over on Acorn."

He nodded with a knowing smile. "Beaker's is everyone's favorite coffee place. See, you're a Ribbon Ridger already."

Ribbon Ridger. She doubted that, but decided right then that she'd like to be. "Thanks, Derek. For everything." She turned and took off toward the break room before she could say or do anything to let on that she was into him. There were a dozen reasons why they should keep things platonic, but after spending the day with him, she was beginning to wonder if any of them mattered.

She could just hear her mother now, "You're dating a server in a pub?"

"Actually, he's a firefighter, Mom. *And* a server."

"What?! Haven't I always told you never to marry a man who wears any kind of uniform? They'll always break your heart."

Right, but marrying a status-obsessed workaholic would've been just fine.

As she pulled on her coat, she thought she really ought to call her folks and tell them about the fire, but they'd only say it was proof she should come right back to Pittsburgh. They'd hated that she'd moved out here. No, hated wasn't a strong enough word. They'd hated that she'd broken up with Ed months after their "save the date" cards had gone out. They *despised* that she'd moved away. To become an *art teacher.*

She might as well have jumped on a train and decided to be a hobo.

Smiling in spite of everything, Chloe swiped a Crossbow tee (and tried not to analyze whether she'd grabbed that particular shirt because it was Derek's favorite beer) and left through the back door. Amazingly, things didn't look as bleak as they had that morning. And she had Derek Sumner to thank for that.

Chapter Three

Chloe drove up to the Archers' house and tried not to gape. She'd been raised in an upper-middle-class family and had spent plenty of time in beautiful, museum-perfect houses, but none of them came close to this. It was clearly a mansion, with a tall stone archway over the front door and a dozen paned windows sparkling across the wide expanse of the front of the house, but there was a homeyness to the design that made it very welcoming instead of imposing.

The driveway led to a turnaround with a water feature in the center. It was built like a natural waterfall and was surrounded by trees and evergreen shrubs. Derek's directions indicated that she should drive past the waterfall and turn right through a porte cochere into a courtyard. Ahead of her was a huge garage with six bays and a tall, arched door at the far right end. She saw a black SUV parked in front of one of the bays and wondered if it was Derek's.

As she pulled her car to a stop in front of the arched door, Derek jumped out of the SUV and came toward her. He rushed to open the door for her, but Chloe just stared at her new, albeit temporary, home. It wasn't just a boring garage. No, the building that stored cars looked like its own separate house with stonework, windows across the front, and a high, arched roof.

She finally looked up at Derek—and he had a good six inches on her five-feet-eight. "You didn't tell me this was a palatial estate. This is amazing."

"The Archers don't do anything by halves," he said, grinning. "Come on, let me show you upstairs."

Chloe grabbed her purse and the small bag filled with toiletries she'd bought yesterday and climbed out of the car. He closed the door behind her and led her to the arched doorway.

"Rob said you can park in this garage bay closest to your door. The remote is upstairs." He opened the door for her to enter, and she preceded him into a narrow entryway. A small, square window on the right at about head level let natural light in.

Light from recessed cans in the ceiling flooded the staircase in front of them. "After you," he said.

Chloe climbed the stairs, studying her new place. It was just a staircase, but they'd painted the walls a warm, comforting caramel color, and she already felt at home. At the top of the stairs was a small landing and another door. This one was open a sliver, so she pushed it wide. A rush of happiness washed over her as she beheld the space. A small kitchen done in granite and dark wood stretched across the left-hand wall, with a slender pantry at the end. A peninsula bar with two stools separated the kitchen from the living area. She moved into the room and immediately wanted to curl up on the overstuffed chocolate-colored couch or one of the cozy, butter-colored chairs. She realized she was thinking of every color as a food and decided she must be hungry. That was her own fault for leaving the Blackbird before partaking in breakfast. But she'd been too excited to hang around.

A small wood table with two chairs sat in front of the wide window that overlooked the courtyard below. To the left, next to the kitchen, was a bathroom. It was small but elegant, with a tiled shower and a tiled counter. Fluffy pecan—or khaki, not everything had to be food!—towels hung ready on the shower door. With a contented sigh, Chloe turned and walked back into the living room. On the opposite wall was a door to presumably the bedroom. Chloe went to check it out and almost squealed with delight at the wrought-iron king-sized bed covered in a scrumptious green and beige quilt and decorated with a good half-dozen pillows. A closet was carved into just half of the opposite wall, leaving an alcove in the corner, which housed a comfy chair. Chloe caught her breath. Cast artfully over the back was a sage green blanket, the same color as her favorite, which she'd lost in the fire. She smiled, amazed at how *right* everything seemed.

"Will it do?" Derek asked.

Chloe turned to see him lounging in the doorway of

the bedroom, his arms crossed over his chest. She suddenly felt very hot just looking at him with a bed only a few steps away. "It's perfect. What do they usually use it for?"

Derek shrugged. "Family who come to visit or whoever else needs it. Rob Archer has a lot of business interests, so he sometimes invites people to stay. As you can probably tell, they have plenty of rooms in the house."

"Yes, I can see that."

Derek turned from the doorway and strolled back into the living room. "Notice anything?"

Chloe looked around and then her gaze was arrested by the painting over the gas fireplace. "That's my canvas!" She rushed over to it and smoothed her fingertips along the unframed edge of the landscape she'd painted a few months ago. "Where did you get this?"

"Your garage. And three more over there." He gestured to a box in the corner with three smaller canvases. "They were a bit water-logged, but they seem to have dried out pretty well. Unfortunately one of them is a bit bowed, but maybe we can restretch it over a new frame."

We? Chloe's eyes burned with tears at his thoughtfulness. "Thank you," she said softly, unable to give her words more volume.

She heard Derek moving behind her, but kept looking at her painting until she'd gotten her emotions back under control. When she turned around, Derek was in the kitchen opening a large box of pastries. Chloe joined him at the bar.

He handed her an insulated cup with the Beaker's logo on the side. "Here's your chai."

She smiled gratefully. "Perfect, thanks." She turned and took in the wall of windows opposite the fireplace. They offered a ton of natural light. She could see herself painting here—as soon as she replaced her art supplies. But she wouldn't be here that long, probably. She had to find a new place in less than ten days.

She shoved the thought away, wanting to focus on how awesome this morning was and how wonderful it felt to be taken care of after the fire. With everyone's kindness and generosity, she actually felt as though she was finally home. Then her stomach growled and she realized she needed to get some groceries to truly make it one.

Derek chuckled. "Hungry? Me too." He moved behind the bar into the kitchen. "Lucky for you, Emily stocked the place."

"She did?"

"I told you she was a great mother." He glanced at the door. "I imagine she'll be over in a bit. She's anxious to deliver your cat, whose vision is already improving, by the way."

"Really?" Chloe grinned. "That's great!" Her stomach growled again.

Derek chuckled. "Let's get you something to eat." He inclined his head toward the large open box in front of him on the counter. A half dozen baked goods—Danish, croissants, and doughnuts—taunted her. "Pick a pastry, any pastry."

After an agonizingly indecisive moment, she pointed at the cheese Danish drizzled with dark chocolate. "That one."

"Good choice. Have a seat and I'll bring it over."

She picked up his chai in her other hand. "I've got your tea."

As she set the cups on the table, she heard him moving about the kitchen, getting plates out of the cupboard.

"So tell me about your art. Why aren't you doing that for a living?" he asked.

Chloe sat in one of the ladder-backed chairs. "I sort-of am. I'll be teaching art at the Cascade Children's Academy starting after the winter break."

"Really?" He came around the bar carrying two plates, which he set on the table. "Waiting tables is just something extra you do?"

"Yes, a part-time teaching job makes things pretty tight." She noted that he'd chosen the raspberry-filled croissant. "I almost picked that."

He froze with the croissant halfway to his mouth. "You want me to save it for you?"

"No, please, you have it." She took a gleeful bite of her Danish and was delighted to find it tasted even better than it looked. They ate in silence a moment before she said, "Where did you get these? They're heavenly."

"Eloise's Bakery. It's actually over in Dundee." That was a ten-minute drive east of Ribbon Ridge. He'd gone out of his way to be impressive and amazing.

"I'm glad it's not in Ribbon Ridge or I might gain ten pounds in my first month here."

He rolled his fabulous blue eyes. "Tell me about it. Our town might be small, but it's surrounded by great restaurants, fine wineries, and of course it has the best brewer in the state. If not for my trainer, I'd be three hundred pounds."

She doubted that; he was clearly very athletically fit. He had to be in order to control one of those high-pressure fire hoses. Though over six feet, he was a lean 175 pounds, she'd guess. She wasn't in terrible shape, but she was sure his abs were far more discernible than hers.

He set his croissant down and took a sip of tea. "So I have to ask, did you move all the way out here for a part-time job at a private school?"

"Yes," she said slowly, putting her Danish on her plate. He'd brought napkins, and she used one to dab at her mouth. "And to answer your next question, sure, I could've gotten a similar job back in Pittsburgh, or at least closer to it, but I wanted a change of scenery. I wanted to live some-where more . . . laid-back."

He laughed. "Oregon's definitely that. Did you spend any time in Portland? It's a lot of fun. I'll take you up some-time. I know some great bars."

A pub guy would know that, of course. "You like working at the pub?" she asked, wanting to know more about him.

"I do. I did it all through college."

It was silly, but Chloe had assumed that he hadn't gone

to college. Neither one of his professions required a degree, but that didn't mean he hadn't gotten one. Ugh, she hated that she'd jumped to that conclusion, as it was something her mother would do. And really, Derek could make a similar assumption about her. Maybe she was just some hippy-dippy artsy girl who painted and waited tables. She smiled internally and loved that whole scenario: artsy barmaid dating a hot pub server/firefighter. Yes, this was the life she'd been looking for.

Spontaneously, she leaned across the table and kissed his cheek. "Thank you," she said, before moving away. "For breakfast, for finding me a place to live, for . . . everything."

He turned his head and caught her lips in a kiss. Chloe nearly jerked back in surprise, but she'd started it. Heat spread from where their mouths were joined and she had to grab the edge of the table for support.

He tipped his head slightly, his lips moving over hers with soft precision. The man had skills. Then the abrupt sound of the White Stripes's "Seven Nation Army" broke the moment and they both pulled away. He pulled his iPhone from his back pocket while she resituated herself in her chair and took a bite of Danish to occupy her mouth now that he'd abandoned it.

"This is Derek," he said into the phone. "Oh, hi. Yeah, I'm aware of that. K. Oh. Well, crap. I didn't realize. I'll be there in a few."

He tucked the phone back into his pocket and gave her a sheepish smile. "I have to go. I forgot I'd promised someone else I'd help them today."

She wiped her mouth again and smiled at him. "See what happens when you try to do too much good?"

"Heh, right. I'll endeavor to embrace my inner bad boy more often."

Heat swirled in Chloe's belly. She could think of exactly how she'd like to meet that bad boy. And the sultry way he was looking at her certainly didn't help.

She stood. "Well, I appreciate the breakfast and everything else. You're my knight."

He stood up too, though she sensed reluctance in his posture and in the fact that he didn't immediately go toward the door.

"Your knight?" he said, finally turning.

She joined him to walk him to the door. "In shining armor. Though I wouldn't mind it if you brought the bad boy out to play some time."

He pivoted at the doorway and faced her, his blue eyes vivid and alluring. "You got it." He looked at her mouth. "Do you mind, that is—"

"No." She curled her arms up around his neck and pulled him down for another kiss. But this one wasn't soft and sweet like the first. No, this time he unleashed his inner bad boy and slid his tongue along her lips until she let him inside. Then his arms were around her, crushing her into his chest and his mouth slanted over hers. This was a movie kiss, the kind that made you sigh and weep and feel hot all over.

After several wondrous moments, he pulled back and gave her a regret-filled smile. "I really have to go. Oh, I almost forgot. Any chance you want to be my date at the Archers' Christmas party tomorrow night?"

A ginormous chance. But she had nothing to wear. Literally. Luckily, Mike had insisted on giving her the weekend off so that she could restock her wardrobe and look for a new place. Step one: find a killer party outfit. "I'd love to."

His answering smile was broad and sent every part of her into a quivery mass. "Great. I'll stop by to get you at six, okay?"

"Can't wait."

"Me neither." He gave her a last, lingering stare before leaving and closing the door behind him.

Chloe touched the door as if she could still feel his imprint on the handle, then turned around and pressed her back to it. Then she heard voices in the stairwell and pivoted to reopen the door.

A petite woman with pale blond hair was just ascending the last few steps, a gray bundle of fur in her arms.

"Ashley!" Chloe held out her arms, absurdly happy to see the kitten she'd only barely met but felt incredibly possessive of.

The woman—she had to be Emily Archer—transferred Ashley into Chloe's waiting embrace. "She's doing very well. Takes her eye drops like a champ."

Chloe stared at her little kitten who was now looking up at her, which she hadn't done the other night. "Oh, thank you so much. It does look as though she can see better, doesn't it?"

Emily nodded. "Definitely. She found the food dish quite easily this morning." She paused. "I'm Emily, by the way."

"Oh, yes, sorry." Chloe nestled Ashley into the crook of her left arm and then held out her right to shake Emily's hand. "I'm Chloe."

"Oh, nonsense, young lady. We're huggers." She reached over and gave Chloe a quick squeeze. Then she pushed by her into the apartment. "I've put Ashley's eyedrops in the cupboard next to the sink there. And there are cat food dishes and cat food in the cabinets."

"I don't know how to thank you—for the groceries, too. How much do I owe you? And for the vet."

Emily waved her hand. "Nothing. I insist. If you can't rely on the kindness of strangers to help you amidst a terrible tragedy, what good is this life?" She continued bustling around the apartment. "There's a litter box in the bathroom. I wouldn't let Ashley outside, especially until she's better, though I wouldn't let her be an outside kitty at all. There are too many coyotes around Ribbon Ridge."

Coyotes? Yeah, she lived in the boondocks, all right. "I think Ashley has had a hard enough time outside. Something tells me she'll be perfectly happy inside as a TV-watching, bon-bon eating kitty."

Emily smiled. "Exactly! Now, did you see the closet in the bedroom?"

"Not yet." Chloe followed Emily to the bedroom,

where she opened the accordion doors to reveal a couple pairs of jeans, some shirts, a jacket, and a sweatshirt. She gaped at the lovely woman. "Did you do that too?"

"Guilty." Though her warm smile said she felt anything but. "I interrogated Derek about your size."

Chloe went and looked at one of the tags. He'd nailed it. Damn, he was good. She turned back to Emily. "I don't suppose I can reimburse you for these either?"

Emily's grin was infectious. "Absolutely not! You're going to have to suffer our generosity, I'm afraid."

"You've done so much. This apartment is incredible."

Emily's face darkened with regret. "I'm only sorry you can't stay here longer, but it's a good thing Derek's house is available."

An inexplicable bead of unease settled into Chloe's spine. "Derek's house?"

"He didn't tell you?" Color flagged Emily's cheeks, but Chloe couldn't decipher what emotion had sparked the reaction. "Well, I'll let him do that. Sorry."

Chloe wanted to ask for more details, but didn't think they would be forthcoming. Emily had clearly said something that she maybe wasn't supposed to, and didn't want to get Derek into trouble.

Problem was—and Chloe suspected Emily knew this and it was the reason for her blush—she probably already had.

Chapter Four

Derek had forgotten he'd agreed to cover a meeting for Hayden Archer. He'd been so wrapped up in helping Chloe, he'd practically forgotten he had a job. And he most certainly did. As CFO of Archer Enterprises, he was incredibly busy and tasked with an enormous amount of responsibility. That Rob had believed in him enough to promote him last year meant the world to Derek and he would strive to never, ever let him down.

After he'd taken care of the meeting, he went to his office, which overlooked a fantastic view of the Red Hills, the tips of which were cloaked in low clouds today. This time of year, the countryside looked mystical, like it belonged in some sort of *Lord of the Rings*-esque fantasy novel.

"Hey, thanks for covering for me, I appreciate it," Hayden said.

Derek turned from the windows as the youngest Archer stepped into the office. Hayden was the only kid who wasn't a sextuplet. At twenty-six, he was just fourteen months younger than his siblings, and the only one aside from Alex, whose health problems required him to stay where he could receive care, who hadn't moved away from Ribbon Ridge. He was also the only one who currently worked for Archer Enterprises, as vice president of Operations. Most importantly, he was a good friend.

"Mom says you helped the woman from the fire move into the apartment today. She hot or something? That why you almost missed the meeting you were supposed to cover?"

Derek recognized the teasing tone to Hayden's questions. "Maybe. But she's spoken for."

Hayden sprawled into one of the leather chairs in front of Derek's desk. "Married? That's a bummer."

"Not married."

Hayden's brows rose. "Oh? Spoken for . . . by you?" When Derek didn't say anything, Hayden nodded once. "Interesting. Didn't you just meet her?"

Derek shrugged, not wanting to draw too much attention to it. "Hey, I have to keep you Archer boys from stealing all the girls. Do you know how hard it was to get a date with Liam and Kyle around?"

Hayden snorted. "Um, yeah. They're my older brothers, remember? But your memory's faulty, old man. I seem to recall you doing just fine scoring dates, so you won't be getting any pity from me."

Derek smiled as he dropped into his chair. Hayden was right, but that didn't stop Derek from flipping shit as good as he got it. "I know Liam's coming to the party, but is Kyle?" Though Kyle had once been Derek's closest friend, they hadn't spoken in months.

Brows dipping over his blue-green eyes, Hayden shook his head. "Too busy starring in his own version of *Cocktail*."

Derek bit out a humorless laugh. "He's no Tom Cruise. When is he going to get his shit together?"

Hayden shrugged. "You know him as well as any of us."

Better, probably. But he still didn't understand why someone with Kyle's cooking talent was squandering his life pouring drinks for a bunch of bikini babes and retirees. He was an amazing chef and could establish himself as a major force in the culinary community. "Emily can't be happy that he's not coming."

"Not at all." Hayden leaned back in the chair. "But don't say anything. You know how she gets."

Of course he did. Emily was practically his mother. She was frustrated with Kyle's aimlessness, not because he was bartending. She could totally get on board with that, if she thought he was happy. But she was convinced he wasn't.

"How who gets?" Rob walked into Derek's office.

"Oh, hey Dad," Hayden said. "We were just talking about Kyle."

Rob's forehead creased and his gray eyes darkened to

storm clouds. "Don't get me started. I can't believe he's disappointing your mother by not coming to the party." He cut his hand through the air. "But I don't want to talk about him. I came to talk to you." He pointed at Derek.

Derek sat up in his chair, responding to the fatherly tone Rob used rarely, but effectively, with him. "What did I do?"

"I thought you were going to offer your house to that young woman? Emily said you didn't."

Dammit. Emily had to have mentioned it to Chloe . . . *crap*. What kind of knight in shining armor was he? "I meant to, it just didn't come up."

"That sounds like a load of BS." Rob didn't suffer fools, or half-ass lies. "She needs a place to live and you've got one."

Derek *had* meant to mention it, but he had to admit—at least to himself—that he'd been procrastinating in the hope that something else would present itself. "I said I was going to do it, okay?" He rarely got irritated with Rob, but he didn't want to be pushed on this.

Rob held up his hands in surrender. "Fine. But if you flake, I'll find her something else. My inventory in town is full at the moment and she'll probably have to go to Newberg." That was nearly thirty minutes away.

"I'm not a flake," Derek said grouchily, thinking of Kyle who *was* a flake.

Rob's features softened. "I know, son. And I know this is difficult for you, but try to think of it as a positive step."

It was the only way he *could* think of it. Really, it

wasn't too difficult. He liked Chloe. A lot. Shouldn't he want someone like her to live in that house? No, because he hated it. He tried to suppress a shiver, but his shoulder gave a slight twitch. "I'll talk to her about it tomorrow. It's a great solution," he forced himself to add, "for everyone."

"Good attitude." Rob nodded at him, pride shining in his eyes and in that moment Derek wanted this to work. He could manage Chloe living there and dating her at the same time. He *could*.

Rob turned to go, but paused at the door and looked back at Derek and Hayden. "Almost forgot. Partial family dinner tonight. Tori's getting in around four, and Evan should be here by then, too. Sara met your mom and Alex at the hospital in Newberg." Sara only lived about forty minutes away, just outside Portland, and came down frequently to help out, particularly with Alex's medical issues. "See you at seven."

"See you, Dad," Hayden called after him. He steepled his fingers on his chest and stared at Derek. "What's up with you and that house? Just get rid of it already if you hate it so much."

It wasn't quite that simple. It was a love-hate thing, and he highly doubted Hayden, who'd never lost a parent, let alone both of them, would understand. "I can't now, can I? Chloe needs a place to live."

Because Derek wanted desperately to change the subject, he asked, "What's the appointment for Alex? It's not his monthly checkup—that was last week."

Alex suffered from chronic lung disease and had

regular appointments to monitor his lung capacity. He was the only sextuplet with a debilitating defect as a result of the multiple birth. Though Evan suffered from Asperger's Syndrome and Sara from sensory processing disorder, their challenges weren't physically limiting like Alex's.

"He's been having some trouble lately. You know how hard this time of year is for him. It's so damp. Actually, Mom is thinking of moving him to Arizona—for the drier climate."

"By himself?" Derek asked, surprised he hadn't heard anything about this.

"No, she'd go with him—just for six months out of the year."

"What about Rob?" He couldn't leave Archer Enterprises. Not because the staff couldn't handle it, but because it was the core of Rob's identity. He'd taken the family real estate business and made it into something far more. Still, Derek also couldn't see him letting his wife and sick son leave the state and not go with them.

"Look, it's just talk for now. I don't even think she really wanted me to know, but I overheard her and Dad talking about it."

"Fair enough." It was very hard to keep secrets in such a large family, but Derek did his best to respect every single one of them, probably because he was still Derek Sumner and would never be Derek Archer—not that he expected to be. Damn, those Archer kids didn't know how good they had it. They had this wonderfully supportive family and they'd all picked up and left town. All but

Hayden, and Alex, of course. And Derek suspected Hayden might've left too, but Derek was sure Rob had applied pressure—probably unwittingly—on his youngest son to stay since everyone else had abandoned him. Why had they all been so anxious to fly the coop? Derek couldn't imagine wanting to leave the comfort and security of a family, but then in his experience, everyone else did the leaving.

Hayden uncrossed his legs and sat up straighter. "What? You look irritated."

"Oh you know me. I don't get why they all left. And I really don't get why they only come home maybe once or twice a year." Except for Sara.

Hayden frowned at him. "You don't get what it's like for them. They've spent their whole lives as a six-person-unit instead of as individuals."

Derek had heard that argument before, and didn't buy it. Life wasn't easy, sure, but in the larger scheme, the Archer sextuplets had a golden ticket. "Yeah, they've had it so rough. Unlike Alex." Who couldn't leave even if he wanted to—at least not without considerable help.

Hayden stood. "Tell you what, you lay off everybody for wanting to go out and find themselves, and I won't tell them what a lame-ass you're being about your house. And yeah, it's the same thing. Don't knock other people's neuroses when you've got plenty of your own." He flashed a quick smile to show he wasn't mad, then took off.

Derek stared at the empty doorway. Maybe he wasn't any better than they were. Actually, he knew he wasn't. He was a mess, not that he ever bothered to look closely enough to see it. No, doing that meant getting really messy, and he wasn't going there.

His mind turned to Chloe and her relocation to Oregon. Was she doing what the Archer kids were doing— leaving home to find herself? She said she'd come here because it was more laid-back. However, he sensed she'd left Pittsburgh for a more specific, more personal reason.

He stared at his desk, but the paperwork he needed to address and the e-mails he needed to answer faded and reformed into the gorgeous face of Chloe English, with her seductive hazel eyes and tempting pink mouth that tasted like cream cheese and dark chocolate. He swallowed. Damn, it was going to be a long day.

And he wasn't even seeing her until tomorrow. Unless he wanted to be a complete nuisance and show up at the pub later. But no, she was trying to learn the ropes and make a good impression. No, he'd bide his time—hard as it would be—until 6:00 tomorrow night.

Or maybe he'd do himself a favor and show up at 5:55.

Chapter Five

Chloe spent most of Saturday shopping for the perfect party outfit and some other items, including a few pairs of much-needed shoes, as best her meager funds would allow. She was sliding some sparkly gloss over her lips when the doorbell rang. She glanced at the clock, 5:55. She liked an early guy. Especially when that guy was Derek Sumner.

Grabbing her coat and then hanging it back up—really, the party was only a handful of footsteps away—she flew through the door and down the stairs. She opened the door and nearly sighed out loud. His black leather jacket was unzipped to reveal a midnight blue button-down shirt. It was a great color on him.

"Hey there, stranger," she said.

"It has been a long time, hasn't it?" He held out his arm in a superbly gentlemanly fashion. Her mother would swoon.

Chloe closed the door and locked the deadbolt, then slid the keys into the pocket of her new black skinny pants. They weren't fancy, but they weren't from Target either. She'd driven forty-five minutes to an outlet mall with some great stores.

He eyed her new dark red sweater, his gaze heating her in spite of the cold. "You look great," he said.

"Thanks, so do you."

"Do you want to walk around to the front, or is it okay if we just sneak in through the mudroom?" he asked, looking down at her. She loved how tall he was.

She contemplated the much longer walk around to the front door. "Is it sneaking in if we're just trying to avoid freezing?"

He chuckled. "Not at all. Mudroom it is." He led her—quickly—to the door leading from the porte cochere.

Her first impression of the interior of the Archer home was the same as that of the exterior: that it was homey, despite its size. The mudroom contained hooks and cubbies with everyone's name on them. Wow, there were a lot of kids, which meant the monstrous house was for more than just show. The floor was a rich brown tile, perfect for coming in out of the rain. Everything was neat and organized, and the pine wreath on the door had warmly invited them inside.

"This way," Derek said. He took her hand and though his fingers were cold, she still felt a warmth from his touch. No one had held her hand in a very long time. She didn't remember the last time Ed had done something so simply romantic.

Derek led her down a hallway toward the sounds and smells of a party. Christmas music filled the air along with the telltale scent of pine. As they passed a dining room on their right, she caught sight of a massive Christmas tree, decked out in sparkling elegance in the corner of a two-story living room. She tried not to gape at the sleigh in the center of the oval-shaped hall that served as a central hub; it connected the entry, the great room, and the gallery hallways leading to other wings of the house, one of which they'd just come from.

"What's that for?" she asked, staring at the nearly life-sized sleigh decorated with garland, lights, and gold accents.

"People bring donations for families in need."

Chloe inwardly cringed. "You should've told me so I could bring something."

He squeezed her hand. "You just lost everything in a fire. No one expects you to donate anything."

Of course not, but she would've. But she also didn't want him to feel guilty for not telling her so she smiled up at him. "I'll bring something tomorrow."

"Derek, Chloe!" Emily came forward. Dressed in a sparkly gold blouse and sleek black slacks, she was elegance personified. She embraced Derek warmly, then hugged Chloe.

"How's Ashley?" she asked.

"Seeing better all the time. She's becoming quite playful." And cuddly. Last night, she'd curled up beside Chloe's pillow and purred softly. It had been a wonderfully soothing and heartwarming sound to fall asleep to—precisely what Chloe needed.

"That's wonderful to hear. And you look so lovely tonight. Come, you must meet everyone." She looped her arm through Chloe's and guided her into the great room.

The party was still young. Maybe two dozen people were scattered around the tree, near the fireplace, and in one of the seating areas near the windows. The sound of arrivals came from the entryway behind them, and Chloe suspected the party would be in full swing before long.

Harry Connick Jr.'s voice blasted over the sound system as Emily led her to the seating area in front of the two-story wall of windows facing the backyard, where a group of five were gathered. At least one of them, a petite blonde, was Emily's offspring judging by her looks, but Chloe wondered if they were all related.

Emily withdrew her arm from Chloe's. "I'll have to introduce you to my husband Rob later—he's working the front door—but for now you can meet the rest of the brood. Most of them anyway. Everyone, this is Chloe English, Derek's friend. Be nice to her," she warned and Chloe felt certain they'd all been briefed about her house fire. "I need to see about the food for a few minutes, but I know you're in good hands with Derek. I promise to find you later so we can talk about him behind his back." She gave Chloe a mischievous smile that she transferred to Derek before she took herself away.

Chloe looked toward Derek, but he was staring after Emily with an uncomfortable expression wrinkling his brow. Not for the first time, Chloe wondered at the relationship between Derek and her—indeed, with this entire family. She was also very curious about this house of his and why Emily seemed to think he'd offered it to her.

"Hi, Chloe." A slender young woman with long, straight auburn hair standing in front of the middle window came forward and offered her hand. "I'm Tori. It's nice to meet you. I don't remember the last time Derek brought a friend to something." She shot Derek a questioning glance. Chloe had to surmise he was quite familiar with this family.

A guy wearing a black sweater that accentuated his broad shoulders and set off his light brown hair stood up from a leather sofa and took her hand. "Hi Chloe, I'm Hayden." He nodded at Derek. "Well done."

Chloe blushed. "Uh, thanks. Nice to meet you."

"Ignore him," said the other young woman, the blonde who was clearly Emily's daughter. "I'm Sara, or number six, if you prefer. This is Evan." She gestured to the tallest of all of them—he even had an inch on Derek. With dark brown hair and piercing gray eyes, he looked a little standoffish compared to the rest of them, perhaps because he was standing the furthest away, but he quirked a small smile and Chloe relaxed. He didn't say a word, though.

"You're the sixth child?" Chloe asked Sara, noting that she didn't look particularly younger than any of the rest. "How many of you are there?" She glanced around the semicircle and counted six, plus Derek. Her inventory also revealed two who appeared to be twins, though she wasn't sure. One was seated in a large, comfy leather chair with an oxygen tank hooked to his nose. The other stood next to him and was the most expensively dressed, with a crisply-starched espresso-colored shirt and perfectly pressed navy slacks. With his thick, waving brown hair, blue-gray eyes, and deep dimples, she pegged him as a heartbreaker, but then they were all uncommonly attractive. Great genes. She glanced over at Derek. Was he somehow . . . related? She didn't see any resemblance, but they all seemed so familiar with each other.

The heartbreaker drew her attention with a pointed look of interest. "You don't know how many of us there are?"

Chloe looked at Derek and wondered what else he was supposed to have told her. "Should I?"

The heartbreaker shook his head with a small smile. "I guess not. That's . . . refreshing. I'm Liam. It's a pleasure to meet you." He shook her hand with genuine warmth.

The twin in the chair smiled at her. "Liam's beside himself that you haven't heard of us. The Archer Sextuplets?"

Chloe looked around at all of them, nonplussed. "Um, no? Sorry." Now she felt embarrassed and shot Derek a slightly disgruntled look.

Derek stepped to her side. "Do you think I name-drop you losers to pick up girls? Get over yourselves." He directed an irritated stare at Liam, and for a moment things seemed tense.

Then Liam started to laugh and soon they were all cracking up. Chloe stared at them, bemused. What was so funny?

"Oh, you poor thing. You've stumbled into an inside joke of sorts," Hayden said. "Fill her in guys, come on."

"It's remarkable you haven't heard of us, given your age," Tori said, still smiling. "We were quite popular for a while there in the mid to late nineties."

Chloe still had no idea what they were talking about.

"We had our own ridiculous television show," Liam explained. "*Seven Is Enough*. The name was a take on that seventies TV show, *Eight Is Enough*." The derision in his tone made his opinion on the entire matter quite clear.

"It wasn't that bad," said the twin in the chair. "And I'm Alex, by the way. He pointed to each sibling as he said their name, "Liam, my twin, Tori, Evan, Sara. And Hayden, but he's not one of the six."

"I'm the seventh 'oops' kid," Hayden said with a grin. "Apparently after you undergo a lot of fertility treatments, you shouldn't assume you're still lacking in the fertility department."

Chloe tried to track all of it. Five of the six were here, which explained why Emily had said "most" of them were present. "So there was a television show about you back in the day?" She tried to recall if she'd ever heard of it, but she just couldn't remember anything like it.

"Yes, and the fact that you've never seen it makes you

the best girl Derek could have ever brought here," Liam said.

"She's from Pittsburgh, that's why," Hayden said. Derek had been talking about her to them. Yes, these were close friends of his. There were so many things she didn't know about him yet, so many things she couldn't wait to learn.

"They carried the stupid show in Pittsburgh," Tori said with the superiority one directs at a younger sibling. As the middle child, Chloe was well-versed in dishing and receiving it. "It was national, if you recall."

"How could I forget? But it was fifteen years ago. " Hayden rolled his eyes. "Good thing Kyle's not here or we'd have another epic debate on our hands."

Beside her, Derek stiffened. She looked up at him with concern.

"Kyle loved the show. He and Derek used to be best friends," Hayden said, accurately understanding the unspoken communication between Chloe and Derek. "Before Kyle ran off to Key West to hang with bikini babes."

"And he didn't come because his bartending job is sooo demanding," Sara said, frowning.

Kyle was a bartender? Not so different from Derek. She found herself jumping to his defense. "Maybe it is. Maybe he couldn't get the time off, especially if he's coming home for the holidays in a couple of weeks."

"He's not." Sara stared at the Christmas tree, a shadow of disappointment over her features and in her tone.

Wanting to lighten the mood, both because her own sadness hovered just beneath the surface and because she wanted to know more about Derek's relationship with these people, she turned to Derek. "Were you in the show, or was that before you knew them?"

Derek nodded slowly. "I was in an episode or two. They'd just started filming after I moved here."

Hayden laughed out loud suddenly. "Oh God, do you remember their tenth birthday episode?"

Derek brushed his hand over his brow and smiled painfully. "I try not to."

Curious, Chloe looked at the siblings, who were all smiling and nodding in commiseration.

Tori sipped her wine. "We had this huge party to celebrate our first decade. Mom and Dad converted the backyard into a mini-carnival."

"I don't think that was Mom and Dad," Evan said, his deep voice breaking into the light mood. Or maybe it was that he wasn't smiling like the rest of them. "I'm pretty sure the producers were behind that."

"Right," Tori said, nodding. "Anyway, there were pony rides too."

"Please, don't," Derek said, his eyes beseeching.

"What?" Chloe looked at him, but he was staring at the floor with a resigned expression. She transferred her gaze to Tori. "What?"

"Derek was afraid of the ponies," Liam said, his eyes crinkling with laugh lines.

"Ponies? You were afraid of ponies?" Chloe asked.

Derek widened his eyes in an expression that clearly said "What?" in the most comically defensive way possible. "I lived in the city before I moved here. The only animals I saw that were larger than a dog or cat were in a zoo."

"We talked him into riding one though," Hayden said, as laughter erupted from both Tori and Sara. Even Evan had cracked a smile finally.

Liam rested his hip against the back of Alex's chair. "Kyle promised him a hundred dollars."

"Though he never planned to pay him," Alex said. "This was before Kyle and Derek became buddies."

Sara and Tori couldn't stop giggling, and now Hayden was laughing.

"Since no one can seem to get the story out," Derek said, "suffice it to say, my first pony ride ended with a dunk in the pool."

The laughter grew. Hayden sucked in a breath. "The whole thing was perfectly captured on film. Derek freaking out on the back of the smallest pony in the yard. Then the pony cantering off toward the pool. Everyone laughing—or yelling, in Mom and Dad's case—and then the pony screeching to a halt beside the pool while Derek lost his seat and fell in."

Chloe laughed along with them, but then stopped abruptly. "Wait a minute. He could've gotten really hurt."

Liam shrugged. "We were ten. Think that mattered to Kyle?" He eyed Chloe closely. "You must be an only child."

"I'm not." And she also understood why ten-year-olds

didn't think about what could happen if they put a frightened kid on an animal, let alone next to a pool. She looked at Derek. "At least tell me you knew how to swim."

"Sure."

"But he faked like he didn't," Tori said, her blue-green eyes gleaming. "He screamed and thrashed, freaked everyone out, even the cameraman. At least twenty different people jumped into the pool to save him. Kyle got in so much trouble."

Realization dawned on Chloe. She grinned at Derek. "You knew perfectly well what you were doing."

He crossed his arms over his chest, his smile radiating a sexy slice of pride. "Of course."

Chloe laughed. "What happened to Kyle?"

"He had to give him the hundred dollars out of his pay from that episode," Sara said, having recovered herself.

"Which my mother made me and Kyle donate to the local animal shelter," Derek said with mock annoyance.

"And after that, they became friends." Sara smiled at Derek in a wholly sisterly fashion. "Best friends."

Chloe moved closer to Derek, feeling a surge of pride for the boy who'd held his own amongst this formidable group.

"I think that's just about enough of memory lane," Derek said, uncrossing his arms and touching Chloe's shoulder. "Do you want something to drink?"

"Sure, a glass of red wine would be great."

He dropped a brief kiss on her forehead and left.

"And there goes the Golden Boy," Evan said. "It's no

wonder Kyle left." As if realizing he'd said something he shouldn't have, Evan glanced down before muttering, "Excuse me," and then disappeared in the same direction as his mother.

"Evan's a bit shy," Tori said. "He'll come back out later."

Shy and perhaps in possession of a faulty filter. She wouldn't hold it against him; she knew plenty of people, her mother for one, who simply couldn't keep their opinions to themselves. Chloe found herself very curious about the friendship between Derek and Kyle and how things had turned sour. She turned to Hayden because he seemed the friendliest so far. "Why did Evan call him the Golden Boy?"

"Because Derek's the best of the Archer children," Liam said. "Well, along with Hayden, the jerk." He lifted his drink in salute to his younger brother.

"But Derek's not an Archer, is he?" Chloe suddenly wondered if he was some long-lost bastard child or something. Maybe that was why he hadn't told her much about the Archers. But that was silly. He hadn't told her much because they'd only met a few days ago.

Liam sipped his drink. "No, he's not, but he might as well be. Of all of us, he has the most drive, the most ambition. Makes Dad so proud. And more than a little perturbed with us."

Hayden shook his head. "Right, because you're all a bunch of wannabes. Tori with her globe-trotting job, Evan with his degrees, Sara with her successful event-planning business, and you on your way to owning half of Denver. Whatever."

All of that faded into the background as Chloe focused on what Liam had said. "Derek's ambitious?" To do what, be fire chief?

Liam lifted one shoulder. "Sure. How else do you become CFO at twenty-seven?"

Derek was a CFO?

"Nepotism?" Tori offered as she brought her glass of wine to her lips.

Several of them chuckled.

"Smart-ass," Hayden said with a touch of heat. His eyes had darkened and she sensed his defenses had kicked up. "Derek and I work our butts off. We've earned our positions."

"Isn't Derek a firefighter?" Chloe asked, feeling rather stupid and hating it.

"Volunteer," Sara clarified. "Most of them are because we're so rural out here. Did you think that was his job?"

That, and part-time serving at the pub, which he apparently only did because he was CFfreakingO and the pub had been shorthanded. Driven? Check. Ambitious? Sounded like it. Married to multiple jobs, including volunteer gigs? Hell yes. Exactly like Ed. Exactly the type of guy she'd bailed on marrying. Why hadn't Derek told her about his real job? Add that to the fact that he was apparently supposed to have offered her a permanent place to live and she had to wonder what sort of game he was playing. The warmth that had nestled into her chest since she'd entered the Archers' home dissipated and was replaced with a cold disappointment.

"Will you excuse me?" She leaned toward Sara and Tori, who were standing beside each other. "Where can I freshen up?"

"There's a powder room down the north gallery," Tori said, pointing to the left.

"Or, you could go downstairs," Sara suggested, her blue eyes crinkling as she offered a small smile. "There are bathrooms at either end of the hallway down there."

"Thanks." Chloe flashed a smile she didn't feel. "Nice to meet all of you. I'm sure I'll see you later."

"What about Derek?" Hayden asked as she turned.

She looked back over her shoulder. "Tell him I'll find him in a bit."

She just needed a few minutes to collect her thoughts. And decide if she really wanted to take a chance on another career-minded alpha dog instead of a family-oriented hot firefighter/pub server. Oh, how she wished that's who he was.

***

Derek walked down the stairs juggling his and Chloe's wineglasses. When he'd returned from the bar, Hayden had informed him that Chloe had left after learning that he was CFO at Archer. She'd seemed weirded out, but Hayden couldn't fathom why. And neither could Derek.

After determining she wasn't in the upstairs powder room, he'd come downstairs to find her.

Later, the party would overflow down here to the bar and pool table or to play poker in the gaming alcove. But for now, it was empty. There were two bathrooms she could use, and he didn't really want to stalk her, so he went to the curved bar and dropped off the wineglasses.

After waiting a few minutes, he heard a noise behind him. Turning, he went into the sole bedroom on this floor— his.

Chloe stood inside, her eyes wide as she surveyed his trophies, posters of the *Lord of the Rings* movies, and the bulletin board stuck with various photographs from his younger years, most of which featured the Archers.

"This is your room," she said, not taking her eyes from the bulletin board.

"Yes. I came to live with the Archers when I was seventeen, after my mom died."

She turned to look at him. Her hazel eyes were dark, her features tense. "I'm so sorry. I didn't realize you lost your mother when you were so young. But then, I guess there's a lot I don't know about you, Mr. CFO."

"Is that a big deal?" he asked, moving farther into the room.

"I thought you were a firefighter. And that you worked in a pub."

He couldn't keep the small smile from his mouth. "And that's better?"

She shrugged. "Maybe. You're just not quite who I

thought you were. You're a super successful guy from a huge, apparently very wealthy family." She looked back at the posters. "Are those really signed by Peter Jackson?"

Derek glanced down, feeling more than a bit self-conscious. He was hyperaware that he was one lucky son of a bitch to have landed in a family like the Archers. "Yeah. He likes Rob's beer."

She shook her head. "That's . . . crazy. You're definitely not what I thought."

Derek moved toward her until he could reach out and touch her if he wanted. But he wasn't sure she was ready for that. There was something between them now. Something he didn't understand. "What did you think I was?"

She looked up at him, their eyes connecting. "A firefighter. A server. A simple guy. I . . . I liked that."

"I'm a volunteer firefighter and an occasional server and bartender. And I'm a CFO. I'm still a pretty simple guy."

"Are you? They said you were driven, that you work really hard."

Derek's hackles started to rise. "And that's a bad thing?"

She shook her head swiftly. "Not at all. It's just . . ." She looked away again. "I'm sorry, this is me, not you."

"The old 'it's not you, it's me' speech? Sorry, I'm not buying it. There's too much of a connection here for us to ignore it." He moved a bit closer and tentatively touched her jaw with the tips of his fingers. "Or am I wrong?"

"You're not," she said, their gazes locking once more.

"It *is* me. Six months ago I broke up with a guy just like you. Very successful, ambitious."

He tamped down a blast of jealousy by reminding himself that she'd dumped the jerk. But the emotion was replaced by a wave of insecurity. "'Just' like me? How do you know?"

"I guess I don't, not for sure. But I'm not interested in a relationship with someone who's driven by their career, who works ridiculously long hours. Status means nothing to me."

He withdrew his hand from her face. "Whoa, status? Just because I lived here," he spread his arms out at the oversized bedroom, just one of many in this house, "doesn't mean I give a shit about that either. I work hard because that's the way I was raised. I love my job, but it doesn't define me."

Chloe blinked at him. She seemed a little speechless.

He dropped his arms and exhaled. "Sorry, but you can't make those kinds of assumptions. Yes, I'm successful, and yes, I'm ambitious. But I'm also lucky enough to be able to pursue those things where I want to be and with people I respect and admire."

Her gaze softened. "You are lucky. And I love that you know that."

"So what does that mean?"

"It means I'm kind of dumb." She blushed. "And judgy. I'm sorry. I shouldn't have lumped you in with Ed."

"Ed?"

"My ex. He's mostly interested in being successful so

that he can buy the Mercedes he really wants or so he can buy a house in Mount Lebanon."

"Mount Lebanon?"

She made a face. "*The* place to live in Pittsburgh, according to Ed."

"Pardon me, but he sounds like kind of a douche."

She laughed. "You see why I called off the wedding."

"You were *engaged*?" He realized there were a ton of things he didn't know about her either and relaxed about her reaction to his job. Maybe they'd felt such a strong connection that they'd both thought they knew each other better than they did. Which was silly. They needed to take this a bit slower.

"Let's back up," he said. He took a step back and held out his hand. "Hi, I'm Derek Sumner. I'm the CFO for Archer Enterprises. I started working for them after I graduated from Williver College. My mom died when I was in high school and I came to live here with the Archers, and I consider them my family."

Chloe shook his hand. "I'm Chloe English. My parents are rather, uh, concerned with their place in Pittsburgh society, which I find exceedingly dull. I graduated from Carnegie Mellon with a degree in design. I'm the middle kid—older brother, younger sister—and I've never quite felt like I fit in. So, I moved out here to find my own place, but, well, you know the rest." The light in her eyes dimmed and she looked away.

He moved closer, running his fingertips down her bicep. "Hey, don't think about the fire. Not tonight."

"It's not that." She looked up at him and blinked. "Okay, it is that, but not for the reasons you think. Do you have a vacant house?"

Shit. The house. He should've broached the subject immediately. "Yes," he said slowly. "I was going to offer it to you tonight."

Her eyes were guarded. "You're not just saying that because I brought it up?"

"No." He wrapped his hands around her shoulders. "Listen, Chloe, I really like you. My house is . . . it's complicated. I'm thinking of selling it, but for now it's a good place for you to land."

She was quiet a moment, but didn't shrink from his touch. "What's the rent? I'm on a tight budget."

"I know. Pay whatever you were paying over on McMurtry."

Her eyes widened briefly and she shook her head once. "I don't want your pity."

Frustration over how the evening was going boiled over. "You think that's what I'm feeling toward you?"

Her gaze locked with his. "I don't know."

"Let me show you then." He drew her against his chest and lowered his lips to hers in a searing kiss, suddenly over-whelmed with the need to touch and taste her and prove she wasn't some charity case. Not to him.

He wrapped his arms around her back and held her close, but judging by the grip of her hands around his neck, she wasn't going anywhere. She met his kiss with the same urgency he was feeling. She felt so good against him, her body pressed into his, her mouth opening beneath his lips and her tongue inviting his into her heat.

The kiss continued for several minutes until Derek realized he had to get a handle on himself before he tumbled her back onto his bed. He broke the kiss and leaned his forehead against hers. "We're standing in the middle of my bedroom, you know."

"Right," she said, sounding breathless. "But it's not like you lured me here to see your fish tank. I'm here of my own accord, and I'm not going anywhere." Her gaze darted to the side. "You don't even have a fish tank. How'd you get girls to come way down here?"

"Wine cellar's next door." He pressed his lips to hers for a heated kiss, then pulled at her lower lip with his teeth before saying, "Do you want to see the wine cellar? It's very well stocked."

"I'm more interested in how well you're stocked," she said, pressing her body tight to his. "Show me the wine cellar later."

"You got it." He resumed the kiss, and she met him with her lush tongue, coaxing him to slide into her mouth. God, she tasted great, like mint and lemon. Fresh and seductive. It'd been a long time since he'd made out with someone, but he wasn't sure he'd ever done it like this.

The feel of her breasts against his chest and her thighs tight against his sent him into a state of full arousal. He held her head and kissed her deeply. He wanted more of her. As much as he could get.

Her hands twined into the base of his hair and clasped

the back of his neck, holding him tight. Maybe it was this connection between them, but every touch felt like magic.

He glided his palms down her back and savored the heat coming through the thin layer of her sweater. She looked and smelled so good tonight. Her perfume was some sort of vanilla and something herb-like, or maybe it was pine. He inhaled, getting that the pine was coming from her hair. When his hands settled at her waist, she pushed into him, her hips angling against his and stoking his desire to an even hotter level.

He moved his mouth from hers, trailing kisses along her jawline. She arched her neck to give him better access.

"I suppose we should go back upstairs," she said, her voice hoarse.

"We probably should." He brought his mouth back up and their lips came together.

Her hands moved down his back and then they were under the hem of his shirt, resting at his waistline. Her fingertips grazed his skin and he nearly groaned.

Taking her lead, he slid his hand up her side and lightly cupped the underside of her breast. He ached to wrap his hand around it and tweak her nipple, but he didn't want to go too fast. Not unless . . . she dug her fingers into his flesh and it was all the urging he needed. He found the hem of her sweater and pushed his hand up inside. She was so hot, her skin soft.

Then they were falling onto his bed. How'd they even get next to it? The last several minutes were a haze. A wonderful, delicious haze. She shifted so that she was underneath him, their legs tangled. She scooted up and he followed, settling his right leg between hers. Her fingers skimmed just beneath the waist of his jeans. He twitched at the contact, his hips driving against hers.

He pushed up the hem of her sweater and bared her stomach. He dragged his thumb across the silky expanse and splayed his hand over her ribcage. Again, he left her mouth in search of new real estate, and this time her neck received his attention as he licked and nibbled at her flesh. She moaned softly and widened her legs.

The Christmas music coming over the sound system in the party area outside his room faded into the background as approaching voices invaded the melody.

Recalling that the door was wide open, Derek froze. The people weren't close yet, but the downstairs bar was only ten or so feet away from his door. He lifted his head from Chloe's delectable neck and saw that she had also heard the voices. Her eyes were wide, her skin not as flushed as it had been a few moments before.

With an internal groan, he rolled away from her and jumped up from the bed. He held out his hand.

She took his hand and got to her feet. "Thank you." She moved to the mirror hanging next to the closet and smoothed her hair.

He went to stand behind her, his gaze finding hers in the mirror. "My pleasure." He grinned absurdly. "Really, my pleasure. That was . . . awesome."

"No regrets?" she asked tentatively.

"Only that we were interrupted," he said devilishly.

She turned, blushing. "Me too. Guess we should head back out there."

"Probably. I set our wine on the bar, so we should defend it at least."

She stood on her toes and pressed a quick kiss to his mouth. "Then you can show me the wine cellar." Her gaze turned seductive and he was pretty sure he could count on at least a mini-makeout session among Rob's collection.

He grabbed her hand. "Absolutely."

So much for taking things slow.

Chapter Six

Chloe felt like she was walking on clouds the next day after touring Derek's beautiful house on Fifth Street. It was an old Victorian with an adorable porch on the front—it even had a swing. But the inside had been completely updated with granite counters, stainless steel appliances, and warm paint colors. Someone from Rob's property management company had met her there because Derek had spent the day hanging out with his "family" before most of the kids had taken off.

On the drive back to her apartment, she felt a touch of regret over leaving the Archers so soon. She liked their family and the apartment was beyond comfortable— despite a somewhat sleepless night caused by repetitive dreams involving her, a super-hot CFO, and a wine cellar.

She smiled to herself, recalling how great last night had turned out. After their wine cellar tryst, he'd taken her on a proper tour of the house, regaling her with a variety of stories about the Archers as they went. She noticed he didn't say much about his own family, but he'd been with the Archers for a decade, and she wondered if it was hard to remember what it had been like before. Or maybe it was too painful. That thought made her sad. She didn't particularly enjoy her parents' company on a regular basis, but she loved them and would be devastated if anything happened to them.

She pulled into the driveway and passed the waterfall. As she drove into the courtyard, she saw Derek's SUV and grinned.

Grabbing her purse, she climbed out of her Civic and went to the mudroom door. She hesitated, waffling between knocking and just letting herself in. Last night, Emily had told her to come over whenever she felt like it—even to raid the fridge at midnight. In fact, she'd wholeheartedly encouraged it since they hadn't had a chance to dish Derek yet, and she was really looking forward to filling Chloe in.

Smiling to herself, Chloe opened the door and walked in. As she hung her coat and purse on a hook she called, "Hello?"

"In here!" answered Emily.

Chloe turned and walked toward the kitchen, but Derek met her in the short hallway leading from the mudroom. "Hey," he said, clasping her waist and giving her a quick kiss.

Warmth flooded Chloe as she smiled up at him. "Hey

yourself."

He looked scrumptious as usual in faded jeans and a cozy green V-neck sweater with a gray tee. Faint smudges marred the skin beneath his eyes, prompting her to say, "How'd you sleep?"

His gaze turned hot as he gave her a pointed stare that lingered on southern regions of her body. "Fitfully." Then he cracked a smile. "Come on, we're having coffee. Or beer. Someone's always drinking beer."

Chloe put her arm around him as they walked into the kitchen.

"Hi, Chloe!" Sara greeted her with a small wave. They had chatted for a bit last night, and Chloe really liked her. She was a little quirky in that she was simultaneously outgoing but also seemed hesitant. Later, Derek had explained that sometimes, especially in social settings, Sara had to work hard to find certain words. It was part of her sensory disorder, but she'd come a long way in conquering many of her challenges. "Come and sit," Sara invited, patting a seat on the bench beside her.

Chloe noted that Alex was also seated at the table and exchanged hellos.

The kitchen included a huge room with a bay-shaped side that faced the back. In the center sat a large, square table surrounded by a mishmash of chairs and benches. A stone fireplace took up part of one wall, and windows over-looking the backyard and pool marched along the back. It was a warm space meant for eating and talking and just being together. It was clearly a central gathering point and even sported a slender Christmas tree in the corner near the fireplace. Over the fireplace hung a family portrait, maybe five years old based on how they all looked. Chloe had smiled last night when she'd noticed that Derek was in the picture. He might not be an Archer by name, but he was definitely a member of this incredible family.

While she'd studied the picture, she'd zeroed in on Kyle by process of elimination. She'd asked Derek what had happened between them. They'd been best friends since the birthday party incident, but then had gone to different colleges. Derek had stayed here in town and gone to Williver College, while Kyle had gone to Portland State University. Kyle had transferred to a culinary school after his freshman year and had done very well. He'd immediately found a position as an apprentice with one of the city's top chefs. He'd continued to find success, but then he'd lost his job when the economy had turned south, and things had spiraled downhill ever since. Three years ago he'd moved to Florida and Derek had barely spoken to him. Not because Derek hadn't tried in the beginning, but it seemed that Kyle had wanted to sever ties with everything in Oregon, including his best friend.

Chloe could feel Derek's pain over the loss, but knew there was nothing she could do except provide support, which she was happy to do.

She took a seat next to Sara, who put her arm around her for a quick hug. She'd already figured out that Sara liked to touch people. As Derek had explained, it was another part of her sensory processing—touch gave her sensory input, which helped her other senses process information.

"Can I get you some coffee?" Emily asked, getting up from the table.

"Maybe she wants a beer," Rob said, winking at Chloe and lifting his own pint glass.

"Actually, a beer would be great," Chloe said.

"Ha!" Rob toasted her before taking a drink. "Marry her, Derek."

Sara giggled beside her, and Alex smiled from across the table.

Derek waved Emily back down. "I'll get the beer." He went to the bar and drew two pints of whatever they had on tap—it looked like the seasonal, but she'd learned last night that their kitchen keg typically held some unique concoction crafted by Rob in his mini-brewery downstairs.

"It's a little similar to the Nock," Rob said, "but there's a rich caramel finish. Great beer for Christmastime."

"Sounds tasty." Chloe noted that only Alex and Sara were here. "Where's everyone else?"

"Liam and Tori took off an hour or so ago," Alex said. "Hayden and Evan are out somewhere."

Derek set the beer on the table and sat on the bench beside her. He picked up his pint and tapped hers. "Cheers!"

Everyone else lifted their pint glass or coffee cup and joined in the toast. Chloe gleefully raised her pint and smiled before taking a drink. The dark beer was in fact caramel-y delicious.

Emily, on the opposite side of the table from Chloe, set down her mug. "So what are your holiday plans, Chloe?"

"I don't know yet." Chloe was all too aware of Derek's heat as his thigh pressed against hers on the bench.

"You're not going back to Pittsburgh?" Sara asked.

Chloe shook her head. "I just left. I'd like to spend Christmas here in my new home." She blushed as she realized how that could be interpreted. "Not *here* exactly, but here in Oregon."

"Oh, I think you should spend it here," Emily said. "Please, I hope you'll consider it. Rob cooks a wonderful turkey."

Alex, seated next to his mom, said, "And Mom makes a mean stuffing and apple pie." He started coughing then, and Emily massaged his back.

When he was done, a moment later, his skin had paled. He was breathing heavily, like he'd run up a flight of stairs.

"Okay?" Emily asked him.

Alex nodded. Chloe didn't want to feel sorry for him, she'd already figured out last night that he didn't like pity, but it was hard not to. She might've felt like the odd one out in her family, but Alex actually was. Of all his siblings, he'd been dealt the crap card. While they were out pursuing their dreams—or flaking, as Kyle apparently was —he was stuck at home hooked up to an oxygen tank. Derek had expressed concern; he worried that Alex suffered from depression, and was pretty sure he was seeing a therapist. Chloe thought that was the best thing for him. She offered him a warm smile and he smiled in return, though it just didn't quite seem to reach his blue-gray eyes.

Sara turned to Chloe as if the coughing episode had never happened. "I hope you'll come for Christmas. We always watch *It's a Wonderful Life* in the afternoon in the theater downstairs. Mom makes special Christmas popcorn—it's vanilla-flavored and sprinkled with cinnamon and nutmeg."

Chloe looked at Derek. "You'll be here, right?"

"Wouldn't miss it." He put his arm around her waist and gave her a squeeze. "You should come."

Scheduling something two weeks out in a relationship as new as theirs was a big deal. Agreeing to a Christmas date was an even bigger deal. But when she looked into his gorgeous blue eyes, she thought she just might say yes to forever.

"Sure," she said, far more calmly than she felt. She broke her gaze from his, realizing things could get a little uncomfortable if they weren't careful. They might be horndogs in the throes of a new relationship, but they were still with his family. "I just remembered I have groceries in the car," she said, which was true, not that they would spoil on a 40-degree day. But she'd been so distracted when she'd seen Derek's car that she'd clean forgot about them.

"I'll give you a hand," Derek said, accurately reading her mind that this was a great opportunity for them to grab some alone time.

"Thanks," she said, getting up from the bench.

"Take your beer," Rob said. "I hate good beer to go to waste."

"And come back for dinner at five," Emily said. "We're having pork tenderloin with cranberry stuffing. I love this time of year." Chloe could hear the contentment in her voice and wondered if her own mother had ever sounded like that.

"Thanks, I'd love that. You guys are incredible." Chloe looked around the table. "I don't know how your kids could bear to move away. If you were my family, I'd never have left home."

At the sympathy in Emily's gaze, Chloe glanced down. She hadn't meant to reveal to them that her family was less than great. The Archers were so wonderful, and she didn't want them to know she came from such a cold family.

"Well, that's a lovely thing to say," Rob said, breaking the tension. "And I'm glad you'll be spending Christmas with us. Your family's loss is most definitely our gain."

Yeah, they were pretty much perfect.

Derek stood up and lightly touched the small of Chloe's back. "Let's get your groceries." When Rob opened his mouth, Derek rushed to pick up their beers. "I got them!"

Rob smiled and Chloe laughed.

"See you later," Sara called as they left the kitchen.

Chloe grabbed her coat and purse and opened the door to the courtyard.

Derek held up the pint glasses. "Hmm, not sure how I can juggle your groceries, unless you want to carry these?"

"It's okay, I only have one bag. You carry the beer and I'll grab the groceries." She hurried to her car and pulled the bag from the passenger side of the car.

He met her at the doorway. While she unlocked the door he said, "You lured me over here to help with groceries. You used me."

She laughed as she walked into the entry and pulled the door closed behind him. "Not true! I never said I needed help. You were merely playing knight again."

"That's where you're wrong. I'm afraid my motives are not at all knightly." He said this with such dark, seductive promise that Chloe shivered.

She turned and led him up the stairs, excited at the prospect of the bad boy coming out again.

DEREK WATCHED THE sway of Chloe's hips on the stairs above him, the curve of her butt beckoning him forward like a siren calling from a distant shore.

He shook his lust-clouded head and somehow made it to the top of the stairs. She set her bag on the counter and quickly put her groceries away while he placed the beer on the bar.

He glanced at the bedroom. *Down boy, take things slow.* But he was having a damned difficult time. She was so great. Everything about her drew him to her, and then she'd said that stuff about her family and how she'd never have left the Archers if they were hers, and he'd fallen hard. She loved and craved a family as much as he did—the same family, which was even more perfect. Last night she'd said he was lucky. She didn't know the half of it.

Chloe hung up her coat and went to the couch where Ashley was snuggled up on a blanket. She nuzzled Chloe's hand and after a moment of petting her, Chloe turned back toward Derek. Overcome with the need to touch her, to convey the emotion bubbling inside of him, Derek went to her and clasped her waist. Then he kissed her intensely, his tongue sweeping into her mouth. She wound her arms around his neck to hold on.

After a long moment, he pulled back, but only a little. She gazed up at him, her hazel eyes slitted with desire. "Wow," she breathed.

Yeah, wow.

"I'm glad you're coming to Christmas." That was a huge commitment. He'd never invited anyone home for the holidays before. "I was afraid you'd say no."

"Not on your life." She twined her fingers into the hair at his nape. "Besides, I haven't had any better offers."

He heard the teasing note in her voice and arched one brow at her. "Is that so? This is a contingent 'yes' then?"

She shrugged playfully. "I'm pretty sure you can convince me."

He knew she meant physically—and he was more than happy to oblige her game—but he couldn't resist being obnoxiously obtuse first. "Well, let's see, it's convenient, for one. I mean, you could shuffle over in your pajamas if you wanted to." He actually hoped she did. He usually spent

Christmas Eve at the house and the entire family gathered in the great room on Christmas morning in their pajamas to see what Santa had brought.

Her eyes narrowed in confusion. "But I won't be here on Christmas. I'll be in your house."

Shit. He'd forgotten all about the house, which shouldn't have surprised him. He'd made ignoring the place a goddamned art form. His heart pounded in his chest and his breath felt short. Overwhelmed with some emotion he couldn't—or wouldn't—name, he left her arms and retreated to the bar where he'd set their beers and took a long drink.

"Derek?" She went to stand beside him. "What's wrong?"

Reluctantly, because he didn't want to talk about this at all, he faced her. "I told you—it's complicated."

She touched his arm, lightly, with infinite care, but it didn't soothe him in the slightest. "Will you tell me why? I really love it, and knowing that it's yours makes it seem perfect. Like we were fated to meet."

Derek wished he could talk about this with her, but he just couldn't. God, it had been ten years. When was he ever going to get over the damn place? "I'm just uncomfortable there. You know my mom died. We lived there together. It's . . . hard to explain." The urge to flee overcame him. "I need to go." He made a beeline for the door, his insides turning over themselves in a decade-old dance of despair that he'd managed to avoid for the most part. And that was precisely why he didn't want her in his house. He should've sold it when he'd had the chance.

"Derek, wait." She followed him to the door. "Let's talk about this. I know we can figure it out."

His hand was already on the door handle and his feet were itching to run. "I can't. Not now. I'll talk to you later." He ran down the stairs and out the door as fast as he could.

Chapter Seven

By 4:30 that afternoon, Chloe was climbing the walls of her apartment. She'd played the conversation with Derek over and over in her mind and was just as unsettled as when he'd left two hours ago. Desperate for a change of scenery, she decided she'd just show up for dinner a bit early.

Again, she didn't bother knocking on the mudroom door of the house. But unlike last time, she didn't hesitate. She went straight to the kitchen where she heard voices.

"Chloe!" Emily smiled at her from the kitchen where she was chopping vegetables for a salad.

Sara sat at the bar opposite her mother. She was slicing a cucumber. "Hey, Chloe. Come and help."

Chloe moved into the kitchen. "What can I do?"

"Do you mind setting the table?" Emily asked. "The silverware's in that drawer." She pointed to a drawer near one of the two commercial-size dishwashers. "And plates are up there." She gestured to a cupboard over the silverware drawer.

Sara set down her knife. "I'll get the placemats." As she went to a cupboard over by the keg bar, she listed off names. "Let's see, Mom, Dad, Chloe, me, Alex, Derek. Are Evan and Hayden coming?" she asked, turning toward Emily.

"I don't know. Set places for them anyway." Emily threw a smile at Chloe. "You never know who's going to show up."

Such . . . flexibility would send Chloe's mother over the edge. "That doesn't frustrate you?" Chloe asked, pulling the last of the silverware from the drawer. She'd grabbed knives, forks, and spoons, but now wondered if she should've maybe grabbed salad forks too. Her mother would say yes. And maybe that was why she hadn't.

"They're all busy, they get distracted, or they get a better offer." Emily shrugged as she chopped up a tomato. "I don't mind. I'm happy to have whoever's here."

Sara laid placemats on the table as Chloe joined her with the silverware. "Sure, but when there's no one here, she's bummed," Sara whispered.

"Sara, don't whisper, it's not polite."

"Sorry, Mom." Sara grinned at Chloe and finished with the placemats before returning to her slicing job.

Emily chatted for a few minutes about this and that, but Chloe was only half listening. She was still consumed with thoughts of Derek and his reaction about his house.

Before she could think better of it, she asked, "Why doesn't Derek live in his house?"

Emily's hands froze in mid-chop.

"Because he has a great loft," Sara said, without missing a slice.

Emily finished with the tomato and swept it up into the salad bowl. Then she wiped her hands on her apron as she looked at Chloe.

Chloe finished laying the last fork down. "Why does it make him so uncomfortable? Is it because of his mom?"

"I think so, yes." Emily came around the counter and leaned against the side. "He doesn't talk about it much. To any of us."

Sara spun her stool around to face them. "I thought he was going to sell it."

Emily glanced at her daughter. "He decided not to, honey." She returned her focus to Chloe. "It's a very sensitive subject for Derek. Please be patient with him. The time is coming when he's going to have to face his past once and for all."

What did that mean? Chloe didn't want to barrage the woman with questions, though. It was bad enough that she was talking to his family about such a personal subject. If Derek hadn't wanted to discuss it, what right did she have talking about it with the Archers?

Emily moved forward and took Chloe's hand. "I can see this troubles you, which tells me how much you care for Derek already." She smiled warmly. "I'm so glad. I think he feels the same. At least, I've never seen him look at anyone the way he looks at you. Or talk to anyone the way he talks to you. It's lovely."

"How's that?" Sara asked, looking at her mother.

Emily turned, dropping Chloe's hand and returning to the kitchen. "How people look when they're falling in love."

Sara made a little sound like a squeal and grinned at Chloe. "That's so wonderful! Is it true, Chloe?"

"Uh . . ." She was literally at a loss for words. She hadn't even considered that she was falling *in love* with Derek, but she was definitely falling in something. Was there such a thing as almost love?

"Oh, Sara, don't put the girl on the spot. It's bad enough I did it! I shouldn't have said anything."

Sara turned on the stool to look at her mom. "Then why did you?"

Emily laughed. "Sara, honey, I'm afraid I was being too motherly. Will you go and tell your dad that dinner is just about ready?"

"In a sec. How can you tell it's love?"

Emily took a pair of oven mitts from a drawer and pulled them on her hands. "I'm not sure it is," she said firmly, with an apologetic glance at Chloe. "I can only say that the way Derek looks at Chloe reminds me of how your dad looked at me way back when."

Sara's brow furrowed. "Doesn't he still look at you that way?"

"Sure, just not in front of you people." Emily laughed as she turned and opened the wall oven. She pulled a gorgeous stuffed tenderloin from the interior and set it on the counter. Then she picked up a long fork and opened the second oven. She prodded something inside, which Chloe couldn't quite make out. "Roasted root vegetables aren't quite done, but almost."

"And what 'way' is it?" Sara asked, leaning forward, clearly entranced by the conversation. It was cute and gave Chloe a welcome reprieve from worrying about Derek.

Emily closed the oven and leaned against the back counter. She smiled, her gaze far-off as if she were seeing the past. "It's a special look. How you look on that first perfect spring day. How you look when the first snowflake hits your nose in winter. How you look when you finish the last page of your favorite book for the tenth time. How you look when your babies are born." She shook her head. "It's a look that perfectly conveys the feeling of joy threatening to burst from your chest, like if you don't let it go in some way, you'll simply explode."

"I hope I feel like that someday," Sara said matter-of-factly.

Chloe realized she felt like that already. Was she really in love with him so soon? How had that happened? She tried to apply what Emily described to her past relationship with Ed, but she just couldn't. Sure, she'd felt something for him and she remembered feeling giddy back in college, but in some ways it was because he was such a big deal. He was one of the top students at school, good looking, and he had the "right" name. That he'd wanted her over any other girl had been incredibly flattering. But it wasn't the same as what she felt with Derek. This visceral feeling of rightness, of wanting to see him at every moment, wanting to share everything.

"Sara, go and get your dad," Emily said, removing her oven mitts. "He needs to cut the pork."

Emily glanced at the clock. It was just about five. And no one else had arrived. She gave Chloe a reassuring look. "The boys know dinner at five usually means five-fifteenish."

Chloe nodded, but didn't say anything.

"Will you put the rolls on the table?" Emily gestured to a basket sitting on the counter, covered with a festive red and green cloth.

Chloe grabbed the basket and put it on the table. "Butter?"

"There's a dish out on the counter over there."

Finding the butter dish, Chloe set it beside the rolls.

"I think you moving into Derek's house is going to help him, though it may not seem like it now." Emily closed her eyes briefly and gently shook her head. "None of this is my business."

"It's okay, I appreciate any advice. I don't really know what to do. I seemed to have met Derek just when I needed to. He's been so supportive—all of you have—and his house is the answer to my troubles, practically a Christmas miracle. It all just seems—"

"Meant to be?" Emily's mouth twisted into a faint smile. "Sorry, I've a bad habit of interrupting sometimes."

"No, you're right. It does feel like it's meant to be. But

then so does Derek. I can't explain it. Things have moved so quickly, but he's amazing."

"He is. Which is astonishing, given his life." Emily's eyes turned sad. "He's had a very difficult time."

Chloe suspected as much, but hearing it twisted her heart. "He hasn't said much about his mom."

"No, I expect he hasn't. And probably nothing about his dad?" Emily asked.

"His dad?" Derek hadn't mentioned his father once, and Chloe had assumed he'd never been in the picture.

"I won't say too much—it's his story to tell—but he lost his dad when he was nine. Gloria, Derek's mom, moved them here to start fresh."

Chloe's heart ached for Derek. She wished he'd told her this, but again, things had moved so quickly, maybe he just hadn't had the chance.

Sara and Rob came into the kitchen just then, and Alex followed a minute behind them. They talked about the pub and how Chloe liked working there and then the conversation turned to Sara's job as an event planner in Portland. She'd organized a lot of last night's party and Chloe couldn't help but be impressed.

She also couldn't help glancing at the clock over and over again until she worried that she would get a crick in her neck. She watched as 5:15 came and went and when the door opened at 5:20, her heart lurched.

But it was only Hayden and Evan who barreled into the kitchen and took two of the open seats at the table. The meal was wonderful, despite the last place remaining conspicuously empty, much to Chloe's disappointment.

It was incredibly inconsiderate of Derek to stand up not just her, but the entire family. Maybe it was her own rigid upbringing, but you didn't say you'd be somewhere and then no-show. Not unless your house burned down.

But his house hadn't burned down. It was whole and perfect and could very well put an end to something very beautiful.

He was such a jerk. Derek had ordered the most expensive bouquet the florist could make that afternoon and had just swung by to pick it up on the way to the pub. The scent of pine and roses filled his car, reminding him of Chloe's hair.

Jerk wasn't strong enough. He was a total asshole.

After freaking out on her yesterday, he'd stood her up at dinner and he hadn't called or texted since. What kind of boyfriend did that? And yeah, he sort of thought he was her boyfriend after Saturday night, not that he'd acted like it.

Then Emily had called this afternoon and made him feel like even more of a schmuck. She'd read him the riot act for not showing up at dinner the night before, which told him more than he needed to know—that he'd disappointed Chloe. Because Emily never took him to task for not coming to dinner. But then, he always texted if he'd said he was coming and then wasn't able to show up.

He parked just down from the pub, plucked up the bouquet, and climbed out of his SUV. On the way to the door, he thought about what he could say to make things up to her, but nothing sounded good enough. "Uh, sorry about Sunday, but I couldn't help wigging out over my old house. I've decided I can't bear for you to live there, by the way."

He cringed because even though he knew he was being irrational, he couldn't help it. He took a deep breath. He could do this.

Pushing open the door, he stepped into the warmth and bustle of the pub. The smell of fresh fries taunted his nose as he looked around for Chloe. He saw her approaching the bar from one of the tables in the back and met her there.

"Hi," he said, tentatively.

"Hi," she said, coming around to the side of the bar and eyeing the flowers.

He held them out to her. "These are for you. Because I'm a jerk. Or an ass. Or both."

"You're neither," she said, surprising him. She accepted the flowers. "These are gorgeous." She smelled one of the dark red roses. For florist flowers, they had at least a nominal scent, which Derek was grateful for.

"The pine smells really good," he said, stupidly, "like your hair." *Really* stupidly.

She arched a blond brow at him, then her mouth cracked into a small smile. "I forgive you. Thanks."

It couldn't be that easy. Still, he exhaled in relief.

"Thank *you*. I'm sorry I didn't come to dinner. That was a dick move."

"Yes, it was, but I understand." She peered at him over the flowers, looking hesitant. "I'm not sure what else to say. You left in such a hurry . . ."

The ball was totally in his court. "I know. It's just . . . the house."

She spoke slowly, as if she were choosing her words carefully. "Maybe I shouldn't move into your house. I talked to Rob last night, and he has a small rental in Newberg that I can afford."

He didn't want her to live that far away. But the alternative . . . Sound, like rushing water, roared through his ears and the floor seemed to move beneath his feet. This was ridiculous. It was a *house*. Where he'd once lived a long time ago. Ten years had gone by since he'd lived there —longer than he'd even called it home. Wasn't it time to let the past go? Rob and Emily would say so. Still, the thought of going there after steadfastly avoiding it for a decade, which was no easy feat in a town this size, filled him with anxiety.

But it was past time for him to get over it already. "Take it." He said the words, but it sounded like they came from very far away. "I want you to," he added, more to convince himself than her.

Her eyes widened briefly, then filled with concern. "Are you sure?"

He nodded, unsure he could get the word "yes" past his lips.

She looked uncertain, but lightly touched his hand. "If you say so." She smiled reassuringly. "I'm going to put these in water and check on some tables. You're not going to run off again, are you?"

He deserved that. "No."

"Good." She smiled before turning and going toward the back.

Derek practically sagged against the side of the bar. He leaned his elbow on the edge and slumped into a stool. His heart was beating fast, and a chill had stolen over the back of his neck. Maybe he needed to see Alex's therapist to work through this.

"What's with the flowers?" George's question startled Derek.

He turned to look at the bartender, whose gaze was inquisitively frank behind his bifocals. "I messed up."

George tsked as he shook his head. "Just flowers? Women are a little more complicated these days. I hope you're taking her to dinner, or maybe you brought chocolate too."

No, but he should've.

"What'd you do?" George asked, pulling a pint of Crossbow and handing it to Derek.

Derek took a drink of the wonderfully cold beer instead of answering.

"Eh, doesn't matter." George narrowed his eyes and leaned a bit over the bar. "Pull yourself together, boy. That girl's the real deal. Don't you dare break her heart."

Derek set his beer down and squared himself toward

George, interested in what the man had to say. "How can you tell she's the 'real deal'?"

"Well, I've been working with her, and from what I saw of you two on Saturday night—all cozy-like by the fireplace—I'm pretty sure you know her well enough."

Derek felt heat rise up his neck. He couldn't dispute George's assessment. Furthermore, he and Chloe had both acknowledged that they felt something special. He couldn't very well pretend she was just some girl.

"Don't forget I'm a good judge of people," George continued, straightening his glasses. "And she's good people. Not like that girl you dated in college. What was her name, Shelby? Gold digger, that one was."

Derek laughed. He'd dated Shelby his junior year and for a while even thought she might be The One. Until George had pointed out that she spent as much time as possible sucking up to the Archers. After that, Derek had kept an eye on her and when he'd found her hitting on Kyle, he'd broken up with her.

Recalling the relationship, he realized it paled considerably when compared with what he was feeling for Chloe. No other woman held a candle to her.

"Listen," George said, lowering his voice, "don't let this one get away. There've been a couple of nice girls the past few years—after that Shelby twit—and you've let them go. I don't know what your problem is, but you'd better figure it out before this one decides she can't wait for you too."

Derek gripped his pint glass as another feeling of—what,

panic?—washed over him. He forced himself to breathe. What was his problem? He'd never considered that he had some sort of fear of commitment or something. He was still young, he just figured he hadn't found the right girl yet. But maybe now he had. And he was freaking out over a stupid house.

It wasn't a big deal. He didn't have to spend a bunch of time there. They'd hang out at his loft and at the Archers'. She liked it there.

Derek realized the bartender was staring at him, waiting for some response. "Thanks, George." He lifted his glass and took another drink.

"Take a risk on this one. You won't be sorry." He stood back with a twinkle in his eye and went to serve a pair of young men who'd just taken stools at the bar.

After nursing his beer a few minutes, he caught sight of Chloe coming back toward the bar. She put an order in with George and then approached Derek. "Thanks again for the flowers."

She was so pretty with her blond hair pulled back in that alluring ponytail when she was at work. It made her eyes stand out and he found he could just stare at her all night.

He slid off his stool and faced her. "Are you free for dinner Wednesday? I'd say tomorrow, but I have a work thing." He flinched a little as he said that, aware that she could be comparing him to her ex.

"I'm working tomorrow night, anyway. But Wednesday I'm off at four."

Happily, he'd started to finally relax. "Great. I'll pick you up at six?"

"Perfect," she said. "Sorry, gotta run." She didn't try to kiss him, but then she was working, duh.

"Have a good night." He sat back down and finished his beer, stealing glances at her now and again as she worked. He threw some money on the bar for George and said good night.

As he walked out into the dark, he inhaled the unique scent that seemed to accompany the Christmas season. Pine and cold and . . . joy. Or at least the promise of it.

He still felt a little unsettled, but reasoned it was normal. He'd just decided to take a chance, to try to face something he'd long buried when he'd turned his back not only on the physical building—the house—where he'd grown up, but on his entire past.

Hopefully it wouldn't backfire.

Chapter Eight

Chloe took a final look at her hair in the mirror Wednesday evening. Derek was going to be there in ten minutes, or five if his habit of arriving early was consistent. When he bothered to show up.

That wasn't fair. He'd been really upset on Sunday. And she could tell that he was still unsettled on Monday when he'd brought her the flowers. She'd been happily surprised when he'd told her to go ahead and get the house, but could tell it wasn't going to be easy for him. She looked forward to being there for him, to helping him work through whatever he needed to resolve.

Her phone vibrated on the counter and she hurried to pick it up in case it was Derek. But the screen showed her mother calling via Face Time.

Chloe stifled a groan and answered the call. She

waited for the connection and then forced a bright smile. "Hi, Mom."

Barbara English smiled, but the Botox kept her face from looking genuinely happy. "How are you, Chloe? You haven't called in a few days and I've been worried."

Was she supposed to check in every day? She hadn't done that when she'd lived twenty minutes away. "I'm good, Mom, just busy. I found a new house to rent, so I've been getting that together." She'd talked to her mom briefly over the weekend and had told her about the fire, but nothing else other than that she was staying with "friends." Probably time to come clean about the job too. "Plus, I'm working."

Mom looked surprised. "But I didn't think you started until next month."

Chloe braced herself for a lecture. "I'm waiting tables at a local pub. The teaching position is only part-time and I need to supplement my income."

Mom's face got bigger on the screen as she moved closer to her phone. "Chloe! You can't be waiting tables! You have a degree from Carnegie Mellon!"

"Mom, listen, it's a really nice place and I like it. The people I'm staying with? They own the pub."

A disgruntled frown turned Mom's lips down in one of her favorite expressions. "Well, I do not approve. You should come home. I'm sure Liberty would take you back."

Liberty Media had been a great job after college, but Chloe couldn't see herself going backward instead of forward. "Probably, but I don't want to go back. Mom, I'm happy here. I met a guy and he's great."

"You just got there! You can't possibly be dating." She held the phone farther away. "Ed was here for dinner Sunday. He still misses you. If you came home for Christmas—"

Chloe cut her off, sounding more stern than she probably ought, but she just couldn't listen to her mother sing Ed's praises. "Mom, I'm not coming home for Christmas, and I'm definitely not coming back to Ed."

Mom sniffed. "He still loves you, dear."

"I doubt that." Chloe doubted he'd ever loved her at all, but instead of it making her angry, it just made her feel sad for him because she was pretty sure he had no idea what the emotion felt like. "But please give him my best. You know what? Tell him I have a new boyfriend. Maybe that will help him move on."

"A boyfriend?" Mom's voice climbed.

As if on cue, the doorbell rang. "Mom, I have to go. That's Derek. We have a dinner date."

Mom exhaled, sounding defeated. "I was going to say you looked really nice. Is that a new blouse?"

"Yes, I had to buy new clothes because of the fire."

"Right." She frowned again. "I wish you'd let me send some money."

"I'm fine, Mom, really. If I need help, I'll let you know." She'd let Dad know. He'd always been easier to talk to than Mom.

"At least let me send you some accessories. That blouse

is screaming for a long gold necklace. You know, like that one with the little crystals I have?"

The doorbell sounded again. "Mom, I really have to go."

"But when do I get to meet this Derek?" No time soon, thank goodness for distance.

"I'll send a picture, okay?" Chloe didn't know when that would be, but she made no promises about that.

"Okay. Have fun. Call soon!"

"Will do." Chloe ended the call, grabbed her coat and purse, and dashed down the stairs.

When she opened the door, she was a bit breathless. "Hi."

"You okay?" he asked, looking at her with a touch of concern.

"Yeah." She shoved her phone into her purse and started to put her coat on. Derek grabbed the collar and helped her into it. Such a gentleman. "I was on the phone with my mom."

"Ah. How is she?"

"Judgmental." Chloe inwardly cringed. She hadn't meant to say that, but why not? She didn't want to hide anything from him. She turned and locked the door, then walked with him to his SUV, where he held open the passenger door.

He climbed into the driver's side a moment later and started the engine. "What's she judging you about?"

Chloe set her purse at her feet and gave him an exasperated glance tinged with humor, because if she didn't laugh at the situation, frustration would reign. "Everything?"

Derek drove out of the courtyard and past the waterfall. "Ouch. That can't be easy."

"No. She hates that I'm waiting tables. Thinks it's beneath me."

"That's silly."

"Exactly. She doesn't understand why I moved out here. I just had to get away from them. I love them, I do, but she's so smothering. Nothing I do is ever quite good enough." She glanced down at her chest. "I'm lacking a gold necklace, for instance."

He threw her a confused glance. "What?"

"My outfit. It needs a gold necklace. But she said I look good anyway, apparently."

"So you never quite measure up?"

Her lips pressed into a grim smile. "Not so much. But then neither do my siblings. One of us is always is in the doghouse for some reason or another. Although, I think it's going to be my turn for quite a while since I left. Especially since I'm not coming home for Christmas."

"I assume that's a problem?"

Chloe leaned back against the leather headrest and sighed. "She really wants me to come home. She also wants me to get my old job back and make up with my ex."

"Wow, she's having a really hard time with your choices, isn't she?"

"Always. My haircut. My car. My love life."

"Uh oh." He cast her a look of mock horror. "You didn't tell her about me, did you?"

"Actually, I did. I said I'd send a picture." A devilish thought struck her and she smiled. "Maybe I'll send her a picture of George."

Derek laughed loudly. "You should! That'd be epic. I mean, unless it would make her head explode."

"It totally would."

Derek was silent a moment before saying, "She sounds like a piece of work. Though I'm sure there are good things about her and the rest of your family, right?"

He sounded hopeful, and she realized how this must sound to him. She had a family, had left them, and didn't seem to want to be around them. Whereas his parents had died. Yes, he had a family now, but it was a surrogate.

"There are very good things about them. They're loyal. I know they care about me. My mom, for all her idiosyncrasies, throws a great party. She would've loved the Archers' shindig the other night. And my dad is pretty sweet. He works a lot though, so it's always been more Mom than Dad. I'm hoping he's going to retire soon. He totally could, but he doesn't." She suddenly felt like maybe she'd been too harsh on them.

"Yeah, I wonder when Rob will retire," Derek said, "but I just don't see it. He seems to juggle work and family really well. I don't think any of the Archer kids ever felt like he was absent."

"That's nice," she said, melting into the delicious heat

of the seat warmer. It was colder tonight than it had been—in the low thirties—clear and crisp.

"Don't let your mom get to you," Derek said, glancing at her. "It took a lot of strength and courage to strike out on your own and follow your dream. I really admire that."

Warmth that had nothing to do with the seat warmer pooled in Chloe's belly. If she hadn't been already halfway in love with him, she was now.

She also sensed an underlying tone to his admiration. A little bit of envy perhaps? She didn't ask because she thought it might be tied to his family—his blood family—somehow and didn't want to push on that front. She planned to be patient. If her intuition was even half right, they'd have plenty of time to understand everything about each other. Maybe even a lifetime.

Derek pulled into town and turned up First Street. "We're going to Georgia's. Hope that's okay."

"That's great. I've heard really good things about it." It was regarded as the best of three—all really good—gourmet restaurants in town. Portlanders liked to come to wine country to eat, drink, and be merry, and Ribbon Ridgers were more than happy to oblige them with multiple offerings.

He parallel parked and rushed to open her door.

"Thanks," she said, as she pulled on her new pair of bright purple gloves. They were a very soft knit and she loved their coziness.

She slung her purse over her shoulder and took his hand, glancing up at him to see his reaction. He looked at her with the ghost of a smile and squeezed her hand. She had to work to keep the bounce from her step.

They passed a Christmas tree stand manned by Boy Scouts. "Hey, you looking for a tree?" One of them, maybe fourteen years old, called.

"Not tonight," Chloe answered, "but I'll be in the market this weekend." She hadn't planned on getting a tree this year—she didn't even have any decorations—but spending time at the Archer house had made her miss the spirit of the season. She was already feeling at home here. Putting a tree in her new house would claim it as hers and set a stake in the ground for her future in Ribbon Ridge.

She thought she felt Derek tense as she spoke to the Boy Scout. When they continued on their way to the restaurant, she asked, "Do you have a tree?"

"I do. But I have to tell you, no self-respecting Oregonian, even a transplant like me—and you—gets their tree from a lot. I'm happy to support the Boy Scouts; I pay them to recycle my tree after New Year's, but we're surrounded by Christmas tree farms. You *have* to cut your own tree down."

She liked his passion on this subject. "That sounds hard. We always ordered our tree from the high-end home and garden store back in Pittsburgh."

"You're kidding?" They'd reached the restaurant, whose door faced the street. Derek opened it wide and guided her inside by grazing his palm against the small of her back. She loved it when he touched her there.

She shook her head. "Nope. That's how it's done back

home. At least by our family. I don't know how to cut down a tree. I think I need help."

He shot her a sly glance as the hostess approached. "Are you asking me to cut down your tree?"

Chloe batted her eyelashes. "Pretty please?"

He laughed. "How can I refuse?" He directed his attention to the hostess and gave her his name.

She showed them to a cozy table next to a stone fireplace in the center of the small building. She set a large book—the wine list by the look of it—on the table along with two menus, which were just printed pieces of paper. The menu clearly changed every day. "Our special is herb-crusted salmon and we're also featuring a truffle mousse. I'll let David know you're here." Chloe liked how everyone called people by their first name. They did the same at The Arch and Vine.

"Is this a converted house?" Chloe asked, looking around at the exposed beams on the ceiling and the archway leading back to the kitchen.

"Yes," Derek held her chair out for her as she sat. "I never realized it before, but all of the best restaurants in town are."

"I like that. There's a lot of repurposing around here, I've noticed. It goes well with the artistic spirit that drew me here."

Derek sat down opposite her. "Some might just call us beer-loving hippies," he said dryly as he unfolded his napkin over his lap.

Chloe brought the menu in front of her and glanced

down at it. But she was more interested in her date than in food at the moment. "You said you were a transplant. Are you a beer-loving hippie by choice then?"

"Actually, I'm from Tacoma." He leaned forward as if he were sharing a secret. "We're beer-loving hippies up there too."

She laughed. "I didn't realize you were from that far away."

"I'm mostly from here. I certainly feel like I'm from here."

"You don't remember Tacoma?" she asked tentatively, tiptoeing around the bigger subject: his father's death.

He shrugged and focused on the menu, clearly uncomfortable. "It was just a long time ago, and I was young when we left—nine." He was quiet a moment, then said, "I think I might get the salmon special. What about you? Oh, and we should get the goat cheese and onion tart appetizer. It's fantastic." He looked up and smiled at her briefly before returning his attention to the menu.

Though she was incredibly curious about his boyhood, she knew he was done talking about it. Not that he'd revealed much. "The filet looks good. I've been wanting a good steak."

"Georgia makes a great filet—you should get it. And I'll order some pinot," he said, plucking up the wine list that was really more of a tome, given its size.

"Sounds fantastic." She wanted to regain the fun they'd been having before the talk about his living in

Tacoma. "I love that a single guy gets his own Christmas tree. Do you do that every year?"

"The weekend after Thanksgiving—not Thanksgiving weekend, that's too early—plus I'm usually wine-tasting." He grinned. "I drive up to a tree farm and cut down my tree."

"By yourself?"

"Once, but usually one or more of the Archers comes with me. Rob and Emily have something like four or five trees in their house, though they get the main one at a special farm with very tall trees."

She leaned forward, intent on him. "And your tree is all decorated?"

"Of course."

"I'd love to see it."

His gaze turned darker, seductive. "Is that a ploy to get to my loft?"

"If you think so," she said, lifting her shoulder and giving him a coy look. "I was pretty successful in getting you to show me your old bedroom."

"Ha!" He laughed. "So you were. If you behave yourself during dinner, I'll consider it."

She was enjoying this game, probably too much. She lowered her voice. "You really want me to behave?"

He set the wine list aside. His stare was positively smoldering. "Not particularly."

Their server—David—showed up to take their order at that inopportune moment. Chloe sat back in her chair and watched Derek talk to him about wine. As she studied him —his eyes, his strong chin, his lush lips—her body heated.

After David left, Derek refocused his attention on her. "Where were we?"

"Shameless flirting."

"Ah, yes. You behave and I'll take you back to my loft to look at my . . ." he arched a brow, "Christmas tree."

She fixed him with her most provocative stare. "I can't wait."

***

The drive to Derek's loft took less than five minutes, not nearly long enough for the car to warm up inside. Derek parked in the garage beneath the building and helped Chloe out of the car. He led her to the elevator, which they took to the top floor—there were only three, the first of which housed a dentist's office, a gift shop, and a wine-tasting room and the second of which contained apartments.

The elevator emptied into a wide hallway and there were four units, one in each corner. He guided her down the corridor to his door on the right and swiftly let her inside, where it was toasty warm. "Can I take your coat?" he offered, shrugging out of his and hanging it on a hook behind the door.

She pulled off her gloves and stuck them in her purse, which she set on a console table, then turned so he could help her out of her coat. She smiled at him over her shoulder. "Thanks."

"The tree's in there." He pointed down the short, narrow entry hall to the main living space. She took a few steps, then threw him a backward glance that said she was very impressed.

"Your place is fantastic." She moved into the kitchen/dining area and he followed her, his gaze lingering on her shapely legs encased in skinny jeans and incredibly sexy knee-high black boots. "I love your kitchen—all the latest stuff, I see. And very loft-y." She smiled at him over her shoulder as she moved toward the living room.

Wide windows spanned the living room wall and in the middle of that wall stood his seven-foot tree, which still looked a bit small, given the twelve-foot ceilings.

She walked past the sectional to inspect the tree. "What's with the wolves?"

"Emily gets each of her kids an animal ornament every year. Each kid has their own specific animal: cat, dog, bear, et cetera. When I went to live with them, she started giving me wolves." They were the oldest things on the tree. Everything else had been purchased since he'd gotten his own place because he couldn't bring himself to pull the ornaments from the attic of the house on Fifth Street.

"Why wolves?"

"Kyle and Liam started calling me the lone wolf at some point. After I'd become a regular fixture at their house —sometime in middle school, I think. They were a pack and

I was the lone wolf." But he'd never felt alone. Not until after his mom had died, and then there had seemed a small part of him that he just couldn't share, couldn't open up. And he supposed that made him a lone wolf after all.

"How wonderful to have that commemorated with these ornaments," she said, moving around the tree. "And you're a Seahawks fan, of course."

He relaxed, grateful to talk about football. Or anything but what might or might not be hanging on his tree. "Of course."

"You will have to accept my Steelers commitment."

He exhaled loudly as if he were incredibly put out. "If I must."

She flashed him a smile. "Your place is the quintessential bachelor pad. I didn't realize you were a player."

He couldn't keep from laughing. "In Ribbon Ridge? The whole town would be on to me in no time. Besides, players have fish tanks, which I don't have here, either."

She turned to look at him. "What? Oh, the fish tank!" She giggled. "But you brought me here to see your tree— same difference."

"Because you asked!" He laughed, then turned back toward the kitchen. "Do you want a glass of wine? A beer? Martini?"

"Martini, huh? This is definitely a bachelor loft." She'd gone back to studying the tree. "I'll have whatever you're having."

He went to the wine rack that served as the base of the

sideboard in his dining room and grabbed a bottle of pinot. She'd liked the wine at dinner, and this was similar.

Before opening the bottle, he tapped his iPod in the dock on the sideboard and found an appropriate playlist. Florence and the Machine piped through the sound system as he opened the wine. He poured two glasses and joined her in the living room, where she stood beside his tree looking out at the view of Ribbon Ridge and the hills beyond.

She took the glass from him. "Thanks. This is quite a place. I can't believe it's here instead of some metropolitan location."

"I like it. It feels like city living, but I'm still in the country. Or sort of the country anyway."

She sipped her wine. "Best of both worlds."

"Exactly," he said, watching her from the corner of his eye. His lighting wasn't at full blast so it cast a romantic glow over the space, bathing her in soft luminescence. She was wearing her hair down tonight, the blond strands grazing the top of her back and framing her face with perfect angles. Her profile was strong, pretty, her lashes standing out and making her look utterly feminine.

She pivoted toward him. "I like this wine even better than what we had at dinner."

"Same winery and vineyard, this one's just a year older. They're from one of my favorite wineries. It's only about fifteen minutes from here. I'll take you tasting there, if you like."

"There are a ton of wineries around here. Plus the Archers' brewery. I'm surprised the valley isn't full of alcoholics."

"Well, there *is* a nationally-renowned rehab center over in Newberg near the hospital."

She laughed out loud. "Seriously? That's rich."

He grinned at her. "Supply and demand, maybe?" Maybe it was the wine, but he was feeling more relaxed than he had since Saturday night. He was crazy about her, and he wanted this to work. He'd taken a huge step by agreeing to her living in the house. But right now, that seemed so unimportant. All that mattered was her, and the depth of the connection between them.

She nodded at the huge flat screen on the wall. "I see why you made the comment about the TV at the apartment—you're an aficionado. That's massive."

"Sixty inches." There was nothing better than a good action movie or a great football game from the comfort of your own couch. "I like being able to enjoy things at home. I guess I'm a bit of a homebody."

"Really?" She sipped her wine and walked over behind the sectional to where a sliding glass door led out to a patio. His furniture out there was covered for the winter, but he still went out sometimes to enjoy the night air. "Nice deck."

He walked up beside her. "I'd take you out there, but it's so cold. I do have a heater," he gestured to the tall propane column, "but we'd still have to bundle up. And probably snuggle."

She turned and looked up at him. "Sounds good to me. Though, I'm guessing we can snuggle just the same in here." Her gaze turned playfully suggestive and she circled the sectional. She sat, folding her leg up underneath her, and patted the cushion.

As if he needed encouragement. He set his wineglass on the coffee table and sat close to her. She held up her glass in silent question, and he took it from her and put it beside his.

He looked at her, drinking in her beautiful face and expectant gaze, and found her far more intoxicating than the wine. He leaned forward and kissed her, bracing his right hand on the back of the couch.

She arched up into him, meeting his mouth with hers and curling her hand around his neck. It was a soft kiss, sweet. Her thumb stroked against his jaw. He mentally scored a point for shaving again before their date.

He angled his head and deepened the kiss, moving closer. She pulled her other leg up onto the couch and briefly knelt. He caressed her hip with his left hand, kneading her, then moved it up beneath the hem of her blouse to stroke the warm flesh beneath. She shivered, but he felt her lips smile.

He pulled back a little. "Ticklish?"

"Right now, yes." She looked into his eyes. "Don't stop, though."

He held her gaze. "Are you sure? I'm not . . . I don't do casual sex."

Her eyes were dark and provocative in the muted light.

"Me neither." She pulled his head down for a scorching kiss. Desire flooded his veins and he pressed her back against the couch cushions. She fell back and stretched her legs out to lie down. The couch was wide enough for him to lie on his side next to her. He splayed his hand over her side before inching it across her belly.

She suckled at his mouth and tongue, driving him wild, her body moving in all the right ways. He realized her blouse had buttons and brought his hand out from beneath it to undo the top few. He moved his mouth to her jaw and skimmed his tongue and lips across her heated flesh. She felt like silk and tasted like heaven.

She tipped her head back, lifting her chin and giving him her neck in an offering he was only too eager to take. He trailed blistering kisses along her skin all the way down to the top of her bra, an ivory thing with lace and gold stitching. It looked like candy—definitely good enough to eat. *And* it unclasped in the front.

Take it slow, remember? his mind screamed. But the rest of his body had a completely different idea. He unbuttoned her blouse entirely and spread it apart, exposing the plane of her stomach. He kissed the tops of her breasts, wanting so much more, but not wanting to rush her. Though, from the sound of her breathing punctuated with sexy little moans, he doubted that was possible. Still, he took his time cupping her through her bra before he flicked the gold clasp.

She gasped as he pushed the cups aside and slid his

mouth down to the tip of one breast. Her hand tangled in his hair, holding him close.

He could feel her desire climbing by the rotation of her hips and the press of her hands against him. That she wanted him as much as he wanted her fueled his own lust. He moved to her other breast, his fingers taking over the nipple he'd just abandoned with gentle rolls and tugs. Her legs parted and she pressed up against his thigh nestled between hers. He pressed it up, seeking her hot center, giving her the pressure she seemed to crave. Her answering moan made him smile against her breast.

"Derek," she said, sounding as breathless as he felt. "Stop."

Dousing him with ice water wouldn't have had the same horrible effect. He closed his eyes briefly as he withdrew his leg from between hers.

But she tightened her grip on him. "No." She smiled, looking a little shy, which he found incredibly adorable. "I don't want to stop. I just wondered where your bedroom was located. This isn't your typical loft with everything in one room so . . ."

He couldn't keep from grinning as relief poured through him.

"If that's okay?" she asked tentatively.

"It's more than okay." He leaned down again and kissed her with heat and passion and whatever emotion was careening through him. Though he was loath to leave her, he forced himself up and offered her his hand.

She gave him a demure look that quickly became saucy as she took his hand. He led her to the bedroom, which was on the other side of a wall from the dining room. A half wall contained a pocket door so that he could close it off entirely, but that wasn't necessary tonight.

She came around him and backed the last couple of feet toward his bed, a sleek platform-style. "I should tell you, I take shots and I'm clean. In fact, you're my first partner besides Ed in five years. I'm comfortable if you don't want to wear a condom."

Wow. He suddenly wished he could claim such a record, but at least he wasn't a manwhore. "I'm also clean, and you're my first partner in nine months. Before that, it's, uh, a bit checkered. But, like I said I'm not into casual sex, not even back in college." Given the precautions she was taking, he opted to skip the condom. "If you're good with commando, I am too."

"Commando is perfect." She tugged his sweater over his head and inched his tee up his stomach, each stroke of her fingertips igniting sparks of need. She exhaled against his flesh. "I knew you'd have great abs."

He grinned, very happy now that he had put up with his once-weekly sessions with his trainer and all the work-outs in between. "And I knew you'd have perfect breasts." He glided his hands up her ribcage between the front edges of her blouse and cupped them again.

She closed her eyes and shrugged out of the top, letting it fall to the floor. The music changed to a sexy song by Maroon 5, perhaps prompting her to stand up on her toes and kiss him, her mouth hot and open. She dragged his tee up his chest, barely breaking the kiss to draw it over his head. And then her bare breasts were against his bare pecs, Adam Levine started singing about losing himself in some nameless girl, and Derek was lost himself.

Chapter Nine

Derek pushed Chloe's bra over her shoulders as she dug her fingers into his back. She felt the edge of his bed against the backs of her knees and let herself fall. The comforter, a patchwork of silk and velvet and luxurious cotton, caressed her as she scooched back so that she was fully lying on the bed.

Though Derek had fallen with her, he'd rolled to the side. Bummer, because she'd really wanted him on top of her. His weight was delicious, his body perfectly sculpted. He felt great against her.

But he was undoing her jeans and she couldn't find fault with that. Without breaking their kiss, she started on his, flicking the button open with ease. Once the zipper was down, she tucked her hands inside and stroked the ridge of his pelvic bone, scrumptiously delineated.

He was trying to pull her jeans down, but they were super skinny and she had to help. Also, there were her damn boots. Reluctantly, she pulled her mouth from his. "Hold on." She leaned down and unzipped her right boot.

"Oh, let me," he said, his voice sultry. "Please."

She heard his shoes hit the floor as he pulled her unzipped boot from her leg. Her sock followed suit, his fingers coasting along her calves as he slowly tugged it off. Then he moved to her other boot, drawing it from her leg with a methodic precision that only amped her desire. When had footwear removal become remotely sexy? Done by the right person, it was apparently one of the most erotic things in the world.

When her feet were bare, he pulled her jeans down her legs—no easy feat given their snug fit—but again he did it slowly and deliciously. Plus, he was staring at her intently, like he couldn't get enough of what he saw. She'd never felt more beautiful.

"Now, these are terribly sexy," he said, inching up her legs and looping his fingertip in the top of her low-rise bikini underwear. They matched her bra and she was quite glad that she'd taken the time to buy at least one nice set of lingerie. Wishful thinking had turned into a lucky move.

He leaned up and pressed kisses along the lacy top. She worked not to jerk her hips, both because it was just a bit ticklish and because heat leapt to her core. He'd brought her insanely close to orgasm in the living room just by touching and kissing her breasts, and now she was moving toward the summit again.

Then he was pulling the garment from her, again with slow, tantalizing strokes, so that the lace abraded her thighs in the most delectable way. Moments later, she was nude beneath him.

"No fair," she murmured as he gazed down at her. "You're still wearing pants."

He rolled to the side to pull his jeans off, but she followed him. "Again, no fair," she said. "You got to take mine off."

He grinned up at her as she tugged his jeans over his hips to reveal his boxer briefs. His jeans came off far more easily than hers had, so she focused her attention on his underwear. Copying him, she slipped her fingertips beneath the waistband, her gaze locked with his. Then she deviated from his example and tucked her hand inside to clasp his length. He was hot and hard and utterly ready. She licked her lips, eliciting a groan from him. With a wicked smile, she pulled his briefs down, but not all the way off. She just couldn't resist teasing him. She lowered her mouth and kissed his belly, as he'd done to her. All the while, she worked her hand along his shaft. His legs parted slightly and she moved her mouth to his hip.

His hand wound through her hair. "Chloe." He sounded like he'd just woken after a ten-year sleep or maybe swallowed gravel. Either way, it was sexy as hell.

Unable to help herself, she put her mouth on him, her tongue sliding over his hot tip, tasting his slick saltiness.

"Chloe," he rasped.

Then he kicked his underwear free and in a sweet, swift move, turned her and moved her up the bed so that he was fully on top. "Talk about unfair," he murmured between kisses, "I didn't get my chance with you there."

"There will be plenty of time for that." *I hope,* she silently added, though as good as she felt right now she couldn't imagine anything else.

His fingers coasted up her thighs and found her core, stroking her folds and settling on her clit. Her hips bucked up, her orgasm coming fast and sure. She opened her legs and urged him to come inside before she went over the edge.

Perhaps sensing her imminent orgasm, he teased her, dragging his finger around the periphery of her clit without actually touching it. She pumped her hips, looking for him, begging for release.

At last, the head of his penis was there and she moaned into his mouth. Then the teasing stopped. He thrust deep and sure, and Chloe splintered into a thousand mind-blown pieces.

He kissed her temple as her orgasm slammed through her. She cried out and kissed his neck, his earlobe, his jaw, and finally his mouth as he began to move inside of her. He filled her so wonderfully, so perfectly. Her orgasm had just begun to fade as another started to build.

She moved her hands to his butt, feeling the muscles there and marveling at his beauty and the fact that he was —for right now and hopefully for a very long time if not forever—hers.

Forever?

His increased speed forced her mind from such

thoughts and she was lost to the rhythm of their bodies and the slide of their flesh moving together.

He moved faster, and she knew he was close. But then he slowed. She moved her mouth to his ear. "Don't stop. I want you to come. Now." There would be plenty of time—hadn't he said that?—for long, drawn-out lovemaking. Right now she wanted to feel him come undone.

And so he did.

She wrapped her legs around his hips as he pumped into her several times. He cried out her name as his orgasm wracked his body. She held on to him as she came again.

As their bodies slowed and stilled, bone-deep satisfaction settled into her. He nudged his head against hers and kissed her slowly, deeply. Then he pulled his head up and stared down into her eyes. "All right?"

"Fantastic." Best sex of her life without question.

They snuggled another few minutes before he finally pulled out. "Water?" he asked.

"Please."

He got up and walked toward the kitchen. Before turning around the corner and fading from view, he looked back with a smile. "Bathroom's through there." He gestured to a doorway opposite the bed, next to another television. The guy liked his TV, apparently. She wondered, naughtily, what he liked to watch in bed. She'd have to ask him that.

She got up and went into the bathroom. Like the rest of the apartment, it was ultramodern and gorgeously appointed. There was a tile shower with two spigots, one regular and one a rain-style that hung from the ceiling. The sink was rectangular and floated on the wall. Two free-standing cupboards stood beneath it with fluffy ivory towels folded on top. There was even a sleek, jetted tub beneath a panel of windows that looked out to his patio. Or would, if they weren't shuttered.

She tidied herself up and saw him come up behind her in the mirror with a glass of water. She took it from him, their fingers touching for a tad longer than necessary, and brought it to her lips. She never stopped looking at him— nor he at her—while she drank. Appeasing her thirst, she set the glass on the edge of the wide sink. "Great bathroom. That shower is amazing."

"Want to get in it?" he asked, with a lascivious grin that made her laugh and sparked her desire again.

"Now?" she asked, thinking they'd snuggle or go to sleep or something.

He turned the water on and kissed her. "Is there something else you'd rather do?"

Energy—and need—coursed through her as he adjusted the temperature of the water. She answered him by wrapping her arms around his neck and standing on tiptoe to kiss him more thoroughly. He moved with her into the shower.

Then he pushed a button and water cascaded over them from above. It was like standing in a warm rain making out. Very sexy.

As soon as his hands caressed her breasts and arced down over her ass, she abandoned conscious thought.

Later, as they toweled off, she reflected that she was glad she'd never had sex in a shower before.

When he was dry, he wrapped his towel around his waist and padded into the bedroom. Unsure, she followed him as she dried her hair.

"So is this the part where we snuggle? Or the part where I throw my clothes on and dash home? Though that'll be much easier after I move. I'm pretty sure I can walk from here, which is great."

He'd been walking around the side of the bed, but when his movements arrested for a moment, she realized she'd screwed up by mentioning the move to his house. *Stupid, stupid.*

She hurriedly walked to him and gently touched his back. "Sorry. I'd love to stay, if that's okay."

He turned and though he gave her a smile, it was weak, and his eyes no longer held the intensity they'd carried all night. "I have an early meeting, actually. It's probably better if I drive you home tonight. I'm the one who's sorry."

His regret sounded genuine, but that didn't lessen Chloe's disappointment. He'd made this date, they'd both known how it would end up—or at least she was pretty damned sure they'd both *hoped* this was how it would end up—and now he wanted to drive her home?

She tried to think of something to say that wouldn't make her sound whiny or clingy. She didn't want to be *that* girl. Then again, she also didn't want to be a doormat. "I understand. But this is a one-time pass. I'm not a dabble and dash kind of girl."

"I get it." He cupped her face in his hands and kissed her softly. "Like I said, my bad. And I *will* make it up to you."

Later, as he drove her back to the Archer house well after midnight, doubt pricked her mind. He'd been wonderfully solicitous as they'd dressed and the whole way home, but he'd also been distant. Was it the house? Or was it something else? He claimed to have a work thing tomorrow that prevented her from spending the night. Was that true, and if it was, would his work take precedence over her if they built a relationship? Before she and Ed had moved in together eighteen months ago, Ed had never wanted to stay with her on a "work night." This, unfortunately, smacked of that and Chloe had to ask herself if history was repeating itself.

As she watched Derek's taillights fade into the night, she crossed her fingers and hoped not.

Chapter Ten

Friday glared at him—blank and damning—from the calendar on his computer screen in his office. Chloe was moving into her house. *His house.* And he should be helping her since he clearly had nothing pressing at work keeping him here. He couldn't even reason that she didn't have much to move because she'd gone to the Archers' storage unit that morning and selected some furniture for the house, which was probably now being unloaded. He could at least have accompanied her and then helped to set the house up.

Cold sweat broke out on the back of his neck as he contemplated such a domestic scene in *his* house. He had no memories of romantic love in that place. His father had never lived there, and his mother had never brought a boyfriend home. She'd dated some, but had never met anyone she'd wanted to even call semipermanent. Maybe that was part of Derek's problem.

He set his elbows on his desk and cradled his forehead in his palms. What a mess. To further compound matters, he hadn't talked to Chloe since their date two nights ago. He'd called her yesterday, but had done so when he knew she was at work and likely wouldn't answer. Another jerk move. Maybe George had a point about him driving women away. He didn't want to drive Chloe away. She was different. Special.

His iPhone rang, but it wasn't her. He didn't recognize the number. "Derek Sumner."

"Hey Derek, it's Chad Thomas."

"Oh, hey Chad, how's it going?" Derek had gone to school with Chad's younger brother. Their family owned a bunch of high-end restaurants in the Bay Area and last year they'd tried to poach Derek from Archer Enterprises.

"Good, good. How're you? Still a die-hard Archer-lover?" Chad was well aware of Derek's close relationship to the family, beyond just the fact that he worked for them. He'd been extra careful when he'd offered Derek a job as their CFO last year. He'd been very respectful, and the offer had been more than competitive. However, Derek couldn't see himself leaving Archer. He realized it wasn't because of the job; it was because of the family connection.

Derek chuckled. "Still, yeah. You're not calling with an even better offer, are you?"

"Actually, I am. The guy we hired after you turned us down didn't work out. We'd still love to have you. I hope you'll at least consider it. We're only going to keep asking."

There was a hopeful smile in his voice and Derek couldn't help but feel flattered.

"I suppose I better then." He said that to be courteous, but he stopped short for a second. Maybe he should consider it. He was always so hard on all the Archer kids who'd left, but they were out pursuing their dreams—like Chloe. And that was one of the things he admired most about her, the fact that she'd broken free and followed her heart in the face of disapproval and adversity. Even her house burning down hadn't turned her around.

"Really?" Chad asked, his tone laced with surprise. "I thought I'd have to do a lot more persuading than that."

"Well, I didn't say I'd take it. I'm quite happy here, as you know. But send me your offer and I'll think about it." Already, the burst of open-mindedness was starting to slip away and be replaced with reluctance. He *was* happy here —at work and in his personal life. He'd just met Chloe and he was very hopeful about where that might go, although she had just moved into his house, a situation that practically sent him into a panic attack every time he thought about it.

"It's on its way," Chad said. "I appreciate you taking the time to consider it, Derek. It's a good offer. Look it over this weekend and we'll talk on Monday. Let me know when you're free to come down. I'd love to show you our facilities. We'll have dinner at Franco." That was their flagship restaurant in the heart of San Francisco.

"Sure," Derek said, his mind a tumult of opposing thoughts and emotions. "I'll talk to you Monday."

"Great! Thanks again, Derek. Have a good weekend!"

"You too." Derek ended the call and tossed his phone on his desk. What the hell had he just done? Nothing yet. He forced himself to breathe. What the hell was wrong with him? He glanced back at the calendar on his computer and froze. It was less than two weeks to Christmas. Shit, it was almost the fifteenth.

Sunday.

He suddenly wondered if it was too late to book a flight to San Francisco tomorrow.

Chloe had just directed the delivery guys upstairs to the master bedroom with the queen bed she'd picked out from the storage unit and was about to close the front door behind them when Emily Archer appeared on the front walkway.

She waved at Chloe as she approached, carrying a basket in one hand. "Hi, Chloe! I brought you some baked goods to welcome you home."

Chloe smiled warmly and was delighted when Emily hugged her. "So, how goes it?" Emily asked as she moved inside. She walked through the dining room to the kitchen, clearly at ease with the house's layout.

Chloe followed, joining her in the kitchen just as Emily set the basket on the counter. "It's going well. Thanks again for the furnishings."

"Sorry I wasn't able to go with you this morning. I see

you picked that dark brown sofa. Good choice, it's very comfortable. And I hope you took the bed I told you about —the queen with the posts." Emily drew her gloves off and set them next to the basket.

"I did. And some of the matching pieces. Oh, and I picked up a cat tower yesterday. It's upstairs in the spare room. Ashley loves it."

Emily took off her coat and set it on the edge of the counter. "Where's Derek? I didn't see his car."

A stab of unease pierced Chloe's chest. "That's because he's not here." He'd left a message yesterday saying he had an appointment with his trainer last night and that he'd catch up with her today or Saturday. He'd apologized again for having to take her home on Wednesday and had promised a do-over. Though Chloe was beginning to doubt that would happen. Maybe she shouldn't have rented the house after all, regardless of him telling her she should. She didn't want to lose him over it.

Emily evidently heard the frustration in Chloe's voice. "Is it the house? I've been worried about that. He hasn't come home all week and that's unusual for him. How did your date go the other night?"

Chloe didn't feel like Emily was prying. Yes, she was a sort of mother to Derek, but Chloe felt as if they'd developed a friendship during their brief acquaintance and thought that no matter what happened with Derek, she could always find a friend—or friends—at the Archer house. "It went great. But he's been distant ever since. I guess he's having a hard time with the house, though he isn't really talking about it."

Little creases fanned out from Emily's eyes as she looked at Chloe with warm concern. "I know I said this before, but please be patient. This is a tough time of year for him, and this year will be tougher than any other." She hastened to add, "Not because of you. In fact, I think you might be the one thing that gets him to New Year's in one piece." She gave Chloe's arm a soft pat.

What did all of that mean? "I wish you could be more specific. I'm not asking you to reveal anything Derek wouldn't want me to know, but I have to admit I'm frustrated. I know there's . . . something between us, but if he can't meet me halfway, it doesn't matter."

Something didn't adequately describe what she felt. She was falling in love with him, and had already fallen so far that there was no way she wouldn't be devastated if things didn't work out. She'd never been devastated by a relationship before—breaking up with Ed had been awful, but she hadn't felt like she couldn't recover, it had felt like a new beginning—and the thought of it scared the hell out of her. Yet even with that fear, she was willing to take the risk with Derek. It was why she hadn't stormed over to his loft and demanded he talk to her.

Yes, she would be patient. Because she felt deep in her soul that he was worth it. Maybe Emily was right, maybe Chloe could help him through whatever it was he needed to get through. She'd sure try. A plan popped suddenly and completely into her mind.

"You look as if you have an idea," Emily said, cocking her head to the side.

Chloe grinned at her. "I do, and it's thanks to you."

Emily looked a bit confused, but shook her head with a smile. "All right then. I'll see about having some of that storage stuff brought over. Will you be here later?"

"I need to run into Newberg to get some staples—towels, dishes, et cetera." She held up her hand to stop Emily from offering more stuff. "I'm fine with buying them, really. I like to have my own things." She actually had a secret passion for kitchen gadgets and looked forward to picking out new spatulas and whisks, as weird as that sounded.

Emily nodded. "I completely understand. I'll see about having the stuff brought over around five or so, will that work?"

"Perfectly." It gave her plenty of time to hunt down what she needed—the list of which included a Christmas tree stand. Her plan was either going to be a rousing success or blow up in her face. Either way, she was all in.

Chapter Eleven

Showered and dressed with nowhere to go but hell apparently, Derek paced his loft on Saturday morning. He'd come so close to calling Chloe last night, but every time he thought of her in that house—his house—his blood had run cold and he'd found something else to do. In the end, he'd sat on his couch, which now reminded him torturously of Chloe, and stared blindly at the TV until far too late.

His door buzzed and he froze. He wasn't expecting anyone. Leaden feet carried him to the entry because he was fairly certain who was standing on the other side: Chloe had the day off.

He opened the door and his heart ached at Chloe's sunny beauty. She wore a cute gray hat over her blond hair and she smiled broadly at him while holding up two cups. "You order a chai?"

Why hadn't he called her? His negligence seemed so awful and so pointless just then. Warm emotion overwhelmed him and he couldn't help but smile at her in return. "I might have."

"Grab your coat. And gloves. And whatever else you need to cut me down a Christmas tree. I really have no idea what's required. Do you have a chainsaw stashed in that swanky loft somewhere?" She made a show of peering around him.

"You don't need a chainsaw. The farms have handsaws. The key is making sure they've been sharpened recently. There's nothing worse than trying to fell a Christmas tree with a dull blade."

"Sounds important." She raked her gaze over him, sending heat through him, particularly to regions south of his waist. "Get a move on, then; I don't want all the good trees to be gone."

He laughed. "It's not like a tree lot. You could literally spend all day searching for the perfect tree. I've had to hit four or five different farms before."

She arched a brow. "I had no idea you were such a high-maintenance tree snob."

He grabbed his heavy winter coat from the hook, knowing there were gloves stashed in the pockets. But he'd need his work gloves for the tree cutting. "We need to stop by my car so I can get my gloves."

"Actually, you're driving," she said, handing him his chai. She turned and started toward the elevator. "I walked over. I figured you should drive since I haven't a clue where to go."

She'd walked over—just like she said she would. From his house. Her house. Dammit, he had to stop thinking of it like that. It wasn't really his house. It was just a place where he'd lived with his mom for what, eight years? It wasn't even the place he'd lived the longest. That had been Tacoma. With both of his parents. Ice pricked the back of his neck, and his feet faltered.

Chloe punched the elevator button and pivoted toward him. "Aren't you coming?"

He heard just the faintest note of uncertainty in her voice and hated himself. Why was he doing this to her? He could either deal with the house—*her* house—or he couldn't. Time to man up.

"Yeah." He locked the door behind himself and joined her.

A few minutes later they were ensconced in his car, seat warmers turned on full blast. He pulled out of his garage and drove out of town up into the Red Hills. He took her to the farm where he'd gotten his tree, but after only five minutes she said, "Nope."

"How can you tell?" he asked. "You've barely looked."

"Everything's too tall. I only want a five-footer or so. I have exactly two strings of LED lights and three packages of cheap ornaments I bought at Target yesterday."

"I think I know where to go next." They climbed back into the car and he drove her to a small farm run by a retired fellow and his wife. This was one of their "down" years, in that the farmer was waiting for his crop to replenish. He had some good trees, but most were too small yet.

Chloe jumped out of the SUV and smiled. "Much better. How am I ever going to choose?"

Mr. Shaefer came toward them with a broad smile. "Derek, I didn't think I'd see you this year. I know you like your trees pretty tall."

"Yes sir, but my girlfriend needs a smaller tree. About five feet or so."

"Came to the right place then." He handed Derek a saw. "Here you go. You know the drill. Tree that size will only set you back twenty-five dollars."

Derek took the saw in one hand and Chloe's hand in the other. "Sounds about right. We'll see you in a bit."

Chloe bounced along beside him as they set off amongst the trees. "Girlfriend?" she asked.

"Was I supposed to introduce you as my one-night-stand?"

She stopped, tugging his hand so he stopped too. "You're kidding, right?"

Ice dampened his mood as he realized she was really—and legitimately—upset. He faced her, wanting to alleviate her concern. He owed her at least that much, but likely way more. "Of course I am. I've been a complete asshole. I should've called you last night. I meant to. I just . . ." He glanced away, "Now, *I'm* a broken record."

She squeezed his hand. "You're not broken. Not as a record, not in any way. I'm capable of being very patient. I know my moving into your old house hasn't been easy. And I don't expect you to be perfect with it overnight. But I'm not going anywhere. Not unless you tell me to—and you'd better be specific. Don't just leave me hanging or I might have to tell the Archers what a creep you are."

"Ouch." He was grateful for the humor laced in her tone. More than that, he was utterly amazed at her supportiveness and generosity. "So I can still call you my girlfriend?"

"You'd better." She flashed him a saucy smile and he couldn't resist pulling on her hand until she came hard against his chest. He stared at her a long moment before kissing her, and that magic he always felt with her wound its way through his veins and wrapped tight around his heart.

She broke away, but didn't let go of his hand. "Come on, it looks like it wants to rain."

The sky was gray, a typical December day, but she was right that the clouds seemed to be thickening.

They looked at the trees and discussed their various attributes. "Too skinny," she said at one Derek pointed out.

"Skinny looks better in my loft," he said.

Her lids lowered briefly, seductively. "I want something with a little more curve."

He caressed the arc of her hip and settled his palm flat against her butt. "Me too."

She laughed and skipped away from him. "Lech."

The next one he pointed out didn't fare any better. "Too spindly," she said. "I like some muscle on my trees."

She caressed the front of his coat, her palm pressing into his chest. "Too bad you're wearing so much," she sighed.

Totally too bad. He was already half-erect thinking about a repeat performance in his shower. Screw that, what was wrong with a little lovemaking among the Christmas trees? Aside from the near-freezing temperature and total lack of privacy. Although the latter was actually a little bit of a turn-on, he realized with surprise.

With that thought in mind, he pulled Chloe against his chest again and spun her to a place between two rather bushy trees that afforded at least a little bit of a screen—not that the farm was crawling with people. There were maybe two other cars here.

"These trees are too thick," she said.

"I'll show you something thick," he said in his cheesiest voice just before he kissed her laughing mouth.

Things sobered pretty quickly as her tongue met his, and soon the heat between them threatened to burn the farm to the ground. She clutched at his back, her body burrowing into his with sweet abandon. He groaned softly, wishing they weren't so far away from . . . anywhere that would afford a modicum of warmth.

Suddenly she pulled back. "There!" She pointed behind him.

He turned and saw a five-foot tree that wasn't too wide, nor was it too skinny, nor was it too sparse. "That's the one?"

"That's the one," she said, her voice tinged with wonder.

He realized she was looking at him, not her tree. The moment held, but then he looked away and strode toward the tree. What was wrong with him? She was perfect. He . . . loved her? Maybe. Probably. Hell, he wasn't sure he knew what that even felt like. But he knew the ache in his chest only intensified when he thought about a future with her. The problem was, he couldn't decide if it was a good ache or a bad ache. He'd only ever had bad ones.

"How do we do this?" she asked, not showing any sign that he'd just ditched a totally romantic moment.

"I take my coat off because this is going to make me hot."

Her brows climbed her forehead and she gave him a seductive look. "Sweaty?"

"Uh-huh." God, he was too lucky. "I lay it on the ground so I don't get dirty."

"But your coat gets dirty."

"Thoroughly. That's to be expected." He shucked off his coat, shivered at the cold, and laid the garment flat next to her tree. "Then I get down here." He dropped to the ground and lay on his side.

"Oh," she said, sounding breathless—perhaps artificially so, which made him smile. "I didn't realize you'd be lying down. Do I get to help?"

"Of course. But sadly, you'll need to stand. I'm going to cut through the trunk halfway and then I'll have you push on the trunk up there to help me cut through the rest."

"Then it will fall down?"

He nodded.

"And who says 'timber,' me or you?"

He laughed. "You can say it."

"Will do."

Derek set to cutting the tree. He sawed for a couple of minutes, then stopped to take a breather. He rolled slightly to his back and looked up at her.

"What's wrong?" she asked.

"Just taking a rest, if that's okay with you, Mistress," he said playfully.

"Oh! Of course. Take all the time you need. Though the longer you lie down there, the more tempted I am to join you and then what's going to happen to my half-cut tree?" She tapped her purple-gloved finger against her lip. "On the other hand, if you go faster, we'll be home that much faster. Where there's warmth. And a bed."

He rolled back to his side and started cutting faster, to the delightful sound of her laugh. A minute or so later, he called up to her, "Okay, push the trunk away from me."

She stood close to him, her feet near his butt, and leaned over to push the tree. "Like this?"

The trunk bent and he redoubled his cutting efforts. A moment later, he heard her yell, "Tim-berrrrr!"

When he got up, she was grinning from ear to ear. "You're right, there's no better way to get a tree!"

He picked up his coat and pulled it on, zipping up the front. "Okay, lumberjill, let's get this tree to the car. You grab the top and I'll carry the trunk."

She saluted. "Yes sir!"

A minute later, they were weaving back through the

trees toward his SUV. He didn't remember the last time he'd felt so good—maybe never. Tree hunting had certainly never been so much fun. He was so glad she'd come to his loft that morning. He didn't know what he'd done to deserve her, but he knew that he'd better figure it out quick so he could keep doing it.

Mr. Shaefer plied them with hot cocoa and little candy canes while the tree went through the binding machine. Then he helped Derek tie it to the roof of the car.

On the way back into town, she chattered about how much better this was than getting a tree back home, and all the while he thought about how today was pretty much better than anything. He was beginning to believe the ache in his chest was definitely a good one.

As he pulled into Ribbon Ridge proper, the ache in his chest intensified and was soon accompanied by that familiar cold sweat. Because he realized where he was going—her house. He managed to steer the car in that direction and as he pulled up Fifth—a street he went out of his way to avoid—his entire body felt like ice.

He pulled into the driveway that led to the double detached garage tucked at the back of the lot and put the car in park, though he didn't shut the engine off. He simply stared at the gingerbread decorating the familiar porch and the barren arms of the dogwood tree his mother had planted.

His throat felt thick and raw. He couldn't speak.

She reached over and touched his hand. "Derek?"

He nodded, somehow forcing his head and neck to

move. "I'm fine," he croaked, but obviously she could tell he wasn't. He didn't want her to see him like this. He didn't want to *be* like this. He thought he could do this, but he couldn't. He'd get the tree down, but then he had to go. He couldn't look at her. She deserved better than some head case who couldn't even *look* at a stupid house without freaking out.

"Chloe, I have to go."

She pulled his hand into her lap and held it. "No, you don't. We'll just sit here a minute."

"I can't. Let me get the tree off the car for you, but then I . . . I have to go."

She was quiet a long moment, but he still didn't look at her. "I'll go get the tree stand."

She climbed out of the car and it was all he could do not to back out and drive away as fast as he could. Just like he'd run off last Sunday. What the hell kind of coward was he?

He got out of the car and turned his back on the house. Methodically, he untied the tree, his heart growing colder and his chest growing tighter by the second.

What kind of coward was he? The worst kind. Because as soon as he had the tree on the ground, he opened the car door to leave.

Chloe rushed inside to get the tree stand from the living room where she'd unboxed it last night. She hurried back out, afraid he might leave without saying good-bye. As she stepped onto the porch, her heart lurched. He'd untied the tree, set it on the driveway, and already had one foot in the car.

Adrenaline pumped through her, fueled by empathy and disappointment. She wished he would stay so she could help him. "You're not running off again, are you?"

He froze when he saw her, his hand clutching the top of his door. "The tree's not that big. I'm sure you can handle it."

She went to the driveway and set the stand beside the tree. "You *are* running away."

His brilliant blue eyes didn't leave hers. At least he had the courage to look her in the face. "It's for the best."

Frustration overtook her empathy. "We have something here, Derek. Or am I the only person who had an incredible time the other night? Not to mention today and every other time we've spent together. You make me laugh and feel things I've never felt before. How can you leaving possibly be for the best?"

He flinched—*good*—and then looked away. "I should've told you before, but I'm considering a job offer in San Francisco."

Nothing he said could've shocked her more. "You'd leave Ribbon Ridge?" Granted, she'd only known him a little over a week, but she'd come to know him fairly well in that time, and she'd seen him interact with his family, which was very telling. She would've bet her insurance check that he would never leave them or his adopted town.

He shrugged, still looking away. "Why not? It's worked out well for everyone else."

Was he referring to just the Archer kids or did he mean her too? "What about the Archers? Do they know about this job?"

"No."

"I can't believe you'd leave them, especially given the way you feel about their own kids leaving."

He looked at her again and she'd never seen his eyes so cold. "This is rich coming from you. Didn't you leave your family for what you saw as a better opportunity?"

She sensed he was rationalizing. She just didn't think he truly felt that way. He loved the Archers. He loved being part of their family. And he loved Ribbon Ridge. "That's not what you're doing. You're running away."

"Isn't that what you did? Ran away from a controlling family and an ex fiancé?"

She sucked in a breath, cold air filling her lungs and powering her frustration. She wasn't getting anywhere with him. She'd been so sure she could make this work, that she could be patient, but if he ran . . . she already felt him slipping away. She moved closer to him and chose her words with exacting care. "Maybe I did run away. But I was running *to* something. I had hope for this life I was choosing for myself. Why would you take this job in San Francisco? You're happy here, and that's the difference. I wasn't remotely happy in Pittsburgh. I'm happier now than I've ever been." She waited, watching for his reaction, but he was stone cold still, his eyes flat in the gray afternoon.

She stepped closer, close enough to reach out and touch his face. "Please don't go."

His expression cracked—just a little—when his brow twitched. She thought she might've won . . .

"I'll think about it." He climbed into the car and shut the door.

As he backed out of the driveway, she wrapped her arms around her middle and watched him leave. She could be patient, as Emily had asked her to be, but not for someone who didn't want to be waited for. And she didn't want to be the one to drive him away from the place and the people he loved most—things he needed to be happy.

Feeling cold, she turned and lifted the tree into the stand. Because it was small, it was easy to get it set, and the stand was built for dummies, with a foot pedal to straighten it once she got it inside. Her heart heavy, she picked up the tree and muscled it into the living room to the corner next to the gas fireplace. She'd expected its presence to make the house suddenly feel like home, but instead it only made her feel worse.

This house had ruined everything. If she'd never rented it, she and Derek would've continued along their joyful path to who-knew-what happily ever after.

She frowned. No, she didn't think that was true. The house was definitely the catalyst for whatever Derek was struggling with, but she felt certain his issues would've come up and been a barrier no matter what. Emily had said it was past time he dealt with things, and maybe it was. Maybe Chloe had just been unlucky enough to fall in love with the right guy at the wrong time.

Could she wait? Absolutely. But for how long? And would he even want her to?

It was definitely his move. She only hoped he would make one.

Chapter Twelve

The next day, Derek sprawled on his couch in a pair of track pants and a college sweatshirt. Even football wasn't brightening his mood. When his door buzzed, he ignored it. A moment later his phone buzzed too. He picked it up from the table and saw the text was from Rob. It read: Open the damn door.

All righty then.

Derek pulled himself from the couch and padded to the door, rubbing his hand over his unshaven jaw. Aside from it being December 15—the absolute worst day of the year—he was pretty sure Chloe would never forgive him after the stunt he'd pulled yesterday, and he couldn't blame her. Now it sounded like Rob might be pissed too. Maybe that job in San Francisco had come at a good time.

He swung the door open. "Come in."

Rob's brows were drawn low over his eyes in an expression of irritation that Derek had only seen directed at crappy vendors or in sticky negotiation meetings. And occasionally at one of his kids. One of his *real* kids.

Rob walked into the loft, not stopping until he reached the bar in the kitchen. Then he turned and gave Derek, who'd followed him, a completely unsympathetic look. "Looks like you royally screwed things up with Chloe."

She'd told them? Derek couldn't blame her. "Probably."

Rob rested his hip against the counter. "She came over for dinner last night—and don't get mad at her, she didn't say a word. However, when your girlfriend comes over and you don't, it says a lot. She is your girlfriend, isn't she?"

"Probably not." Because of his own stupidity.

"What the hell kind of answer is that?" Now Rob *did* look pissed. He crossed his arms over his chest. "Look, I've never said anything about the other girls you were foolish enough to let go, but this one is special. She could very well be The One, and you're getting in your own damned way. Knock it off."

"Thanks, but I don't remember asking for any advice." Derek moved through the dining room, intent on the beer he'd left on his coffee table.

"Too bad." It sounded like Rob was following him, but Derek didn't turn. "I've tried to be a father figure and dishing out advice, especially when it's unwanted, is a father's job. But, I realize I'm not your father. You had a father—do you even remember that?"

The question hit Derek in the back like an arrow. How

could he ever forget? And today of all days, the day his father had been shot and killed in the line of duty.

Derek spun, anger pushing through his veins, but he didn't say anything. He didn't see Rob, he saw his dad. He'd been really tall—that's where Derek had gotten his height—imposing. He must've made one hell of a police officer. Derek remembered that he worked out, and the result was that he sported a badass build. But for all the tough guy looks, he laughed a lot and he had these little lines around his eyes, blue like Derek's, and around his mouth. Derek remembered that mouth reading to him—every night that he wasn't on shift—and shouting encouragement at his baseball games. His work schedule hadn't allowed him to coach, but he'd come to at least one inning of every single game. Most of all, Derek remembered camping alone with his dad. They'd gone just twice before he'd been killed, but those two weekends were emblazoned in Derek's brain like they'd happened yesterday. Just the two of them. Men against the world. Father and son.

Air was having trouble finding its way into Derek's lungs. His throat was viciously tight, his chest constricted. Because after all of that, he remembered the grief. Not just his, but his mom's. To say she'd been devastated by her husband's death would be an understatement. Derek knew, now that he knew love—and he was definitely in love with Chloe—that his mother had never gotten over it.

"Yes, I remember," Derek finally said, his voice sounding like sandpaper.

"You've never dealt with his death," Rob said quietly,

looking at the floor. "And when your mom died, you didn't really deal with that either."

He hadn't. She'd been sick with the cancer a long time and when she'd died, it had been a kind of relief, which only made him feel guilty. And seventeen-year-old boys were pretty shitty at feeling guilty, so he'd shoved it all away to deal with at a future time. Only he'd never let that time come.

Derek's eyes had lost their focus, and when he shook himself to come back to the present, he saw an envelope in Rob's extended hand.

"I know this is a tough day, son. And yes, I think of you as my son—it's an honor and a privilege." He took a deep breath. "This is a letter from your mom. She wanted you to open it on December fifteenth in 2019. But Emily and I think you should open it now. We don't know what it says, but it's time for you to heal and maybe this will help."

Or maybe it would only make him hurt more. Derek stared at the envelope while his insides churned and a light-headedness pervaded his brain.

By some miracle, he reached out, as if in slow motion, and took the letter.

Rob's hand clasped his shoulder. Derek wanted to hug him, but he couldn't. Everything felt too raw, too damned exposed. He settled for giving him a slight nod.

"Call me if you need anything. *Anything*." He dropped his hand and pivoted to go. "You'll get through this. With Chloe if you'll let her. She's a great girl."

Derek stared at the letter in his hand, vaguely aware

that Rob had let himself out. Slowly, he took himself into the bedroom and dropped onto the edge of his bed. With trembling fingers, he split the seal and opened the letter. A small paper fell and fluttered into his lap, but his gaze was locked on the familiar handwriting of his mother. She'd been an elementary school teacher, so her letters were beautiful, perfectly formed. He hadn't seen her writing in years and the reaction it provoked was visceral. Tears pricked his eyes and his throat tightened further.

Dear Derek,

You are as old today as your father was the day he died. I know how much you hate this day, how hard we worked every year to do something to keep our minds off it. It was both a blessing for it to be at Christmas time, because there was usually something to occupy us, and, of course, a curse because Christmas was forever tainted with our loss.

I owe you an apology. I wasn't the best mom after he died. You probably know that by now, you're a smart boy. No, you're a smart man now. How I wish I could be there to see it. Maybe you're even a father now, too. How I wish I could see that even more. You will, without a doubt, be a wonderful father. How do I know this? Because you had the very best teacher.

You're like him in so many ways. Your kindness, your sense of humor, your athleticism, your love of reading. I hope you still write poems. Yes, I knew you wrote them, even in high school. I don't know why you hid them.

They're a gift that should be shared. Which is why I'm giving you this poem that your father wrote. I don't know if you remember it from when you were little. He used to recite it to you when you were very small. It never fails to make me smile because it beautifully captures the two men I've loved most in this world.

Know that we are looking down on you with pride and love. Be happy, Derek. Be loved.

Mom

Silent tears had tracked down Derek's face, and one dropped onto his lap, next to the paper that had fallen there. The poem.

He picked it up, his heart twisting at the handwriting, which he hadn't seen in decades.

> Little Man
> Little hands
> Little feet
> Little mouth
> Big cry
>
> Little sigh
> Little smile
> Little gurgle
> Big yawn
>
> Little sleep
> Little knowledge

Little confidence
Big love

Big change
Big responsibility
Big happiness
Little Man—I love you.

Derek lifted his face as tears flowed down his cheeks unchecked. He didn't remember the last time he'd cried. His throat was still tight, but his chest was loosening, air was coming back to him. The hole in his heart seemed to be shrinking.

He didn't know how long he sat there, but he finally set the letter and the poem on his nightstand. Then he wiped his hands over his face and ran into the stubble on his jaw. He had to look like hell.

And he definitely couldn't look like hell for what he had planned. This day had been full of pain and misery for far too long. It was time for this day to be filled with joy.

Chapter Thirteen

Chloe's little tree was shaping up. Yesterday, she'd decorated it with the lights and ornaments she'd gotten at Target, but it had still seemed a little sparse. Then she'd gone to the Archers' for dinner—her house had just seemed too sad and lonely after Derek's disappearing act—and they'd had a batch of Emily's holiday popcorn that Sara had told her about. That had given Chloe the idea to string popcorn on her tree, although pieces kept disappearing from the bowl beside her on the couch as Ashley artfully scooped them out and batted them around the room. *Love Actually* played on the TV, thanks to Emily loaning her a DVD player and a collection of holiday movies since the cable service hadn't been installed yet.

Dinner with the Archers had been lovely. Any worry Chloe might've had that she couldn't be friends with them if things fell through with Derek had evaporated. It certainly looked and felt like things weren't going to work out, and she hadn't felt awkward around them at all. She only hoped they felt the same after they realized she and Derek were kaput.

Would he really move to San Francisco? She'd spent last evening trying to reason that out in her mind, but it just didn't make sense. It would be far easier for him to cut her out of his life than to run away from his home. And she planned to tell him that.

Now that she thought about it, she thought the Archers might turn their backs on her, especially after she dumped their almost-adopted-kid.

A knock on the door nearly made her drop her popcorn string. She turned and looked through the window out onto the porch, but she couldn't see who was at the door, nor could she see a car in the driveway.

She set the string down on the couch and got up. She could see it was Derek through the glass panes at the top of the door. Joy ripped through her before she tamped it down with cold, hard reason: he was probably here to break up for real.

Swallowing, she opened the door. "Hi."

It was raining, and he was wet. Had he walked over? She glanced at the driveway again and verified that it was empty. Her car was in the garage.

His face looked a bit pale. His blue eyes shone bright despite the shadow of the porch. "Can I come in?"

Chloe's heart was racing, but she forced herself to

remain calm. He could be here for the best of reasons—or the worst. "Sure." She held the door wide and let him in.

He tentatively stepped over the threshold and slowly wiped his feet on the mat she'd picked up during her shopping spree.

"Can I take your coat?" she offered.

Wordlessly, he slipped it off and handed it to her. It was sopping wet, so she just hung it over one of the dining room chairs and let it drip on the hardwood. She'd clean it up later.

She kept sneaking looks at him, but for now, he was simply staring into the living room—at the Christmas tree.

She came up beside him, moving softly because she didn't want to spook him. He seemed like he was maybe only half there. It had to have taken a Herculean effort to even come here, let alone come inside. She would take this as slow as he wanted. She just hoped he wanted.

"It's shaping up," she said, gesturing to the tree. "I'm making popcorn strings. Do you want to help?"

He shook his head immediately. His quick denial iced the hope in Chloe's chest. "Do you mind if I look around?" He turned his head to look down at her. "Alone?"

"Not at all. Do whatever you need to." *Please, just don't leave again.*

He nodded, again seeming like he wasn't really with her, and walked through the living room to the hallway that led to the stairs and the back of the house. She heard him climb the stairs and forced herself to sit on the couch.

Time stretched, during which she neither picked up her popcorn string nor paid any attention to the television.

Emily had sent over a little mantel clock for the fireplace, and Chloe couldn't stop looking at it. Five minutes. Ten. Silence. Finally, after fifteen minutes, she couldn't stand it any longer. She got up and walked to the stairs. Then stopped. She shouldn't intrude. She could be patient.

After pacing the little hallway across from the open kitchen and staring at the clock on the microwave for another three minutes, she gave up on being patient and climbed the stairs. There was a landing halfway up where the stairs switched back to the upper floor. It contained a large window with a seat she'd made cozy with several throw pillows and the sage green blanket from the Archers' apartment, which she'd somehow gotten the guts to ask if she could have. Just seeing it there—here—made her realize you *could* start over again. She only hoped Derek could see it too.

She climbed the rest of the way and paused. Where would he be? There were two bedrooms at the front of the house and the master suite at the back. Intuition told her to move to the front. Still, she didn't move. She didn't want to intrude. Torn between retreating downstairs and continuing, she decided to give him the choice. "Derek?" she called softly. If he answered, she'd go to him. If he didn't, she'd try to mind her own beeswax.

"In here," came his response. Relief flooded her and she realized she'd been holding her breath.

She followed the sound of his voice and found him cross-legged on the floor of the bedroom on the right. The bedrooms were mirror images of each other, right down to the built-in window seats.

One of the boards on the front of the seat had been loosened. Two stacks of paper and a notebook sat on the floor next to Derek.

He looked up at her, his eyes as bright as she'd ever seen them. And she realized it was because they glistened with tears. "These are mine."

Because he hadn't told her to go away, she moved slowly toward him. "What are they?"

"Poems. I wrote them after we moved here." He laughed—he actually laughed. "I sound a little angry."

"Really?" She kneeled beside him. "Do you mind if I sit?"

"Please." He held up one of the papers and read, "Life sucks. People suck. Everything sucks. Except bacon. Bacon does not suck."

She laughed with him. "I have to agree. Bacon does indeed not suck."

He shook his head, set the paper aside, and picked up another. "Home is a four-letter word. I think it's not a good one."

Chloe's heart threatened to split in two. "How old were you when you wrote that?"

"Ten, I think?" He stared at the paper a moment longer then set it in the pile. "We'd lived here about a year. I hated it."

It took everything she had not to touch him, to ease his pain. "But I thought you fell in love with Ribbon Ridge. You made friends with the Archers, right? You and Kyle became best friends."

"Not at first. At first, I tried to beat him up." He shook his head, as if he couldn't quite believe he'd done that. "I did manage to give him a bloody nose."

She clapped her hand over her mouth. "You didn't."

He nodded, a smile playing around his lips, and she nearly threw herself at him because she wanted so badly for him to be happy. "He made fun of my haircut. I'd gotten a crew cut like my dad used to have. He was a cop."

It was the first thing he'd told her about his dad. She regarded this as massive progress, but tried not to get too excited. "That's nice. Not that Kyle made fun of you, but that you wore your hair like your dad."

His smile faded. "I grew it out and I never cut it that short again."

She ached to give him comfort, but she was too afraid to break the moment for him. Instead she said, "But you found your place here."

"Eventually. I didn't make things easy when I first moved here. I was pretty pissy. Hated school. Hated this tiny, lame town." He looked around the room, distaste creasing his features. "Hated this house."

She waited for him to say more, willing patience to outweigh her curiosity.

"It was so quiet. Dad was loud, funny. Always talking,

reading, doing. He was the light and core of our family and when he died, I think it—our family—died with him."

This house was a tangible reminder of the loss he'd suffered. The loss he was still trying to let go. She suddenly wished she'd listened to the warning signs and never rented it. She loved him, wanted a future with him, and if they couldn't do it with this house, she'd move out. "I'll move. Newberg's not that far." She looked at him expectantly, her heart in her throat. "Unless it's too late."

He smiled weakly and reached out to take her hand. His fingers were cold, but strong. "It's not. At least for me. But maybe it is for you. I've been such a jerk."

"It's definitely not too late for me." She appreciated his acknowledging his behavior. "And I've tried to understand. Though I can't imagine how it must feel to lose both of your parents, and when you were so young."

He squeezed her hand. "I miss them." His jaw tightened and anguish lined his face. "So much. And yet I'm lucky to have what I have. I'm not alone. I've never been alone. So why do I feel like I am?"

Chloe couldn't stand it anymore; she moved closer to him, her knees pressed against his thigh, and wrapped her arms around his neck. "Because in some ways you're still the little boy who lost his parents. And you always will be. It's part of who you are, and instead of hiding him away, maybe you should invite him in."

Tears leaked from her eyes as she held on to him tightly, for him, for her, for their future together—she hoped.

After a long moment, he drew a ragged breath. He turned his head and kissed her forehead. "You're beyond amazing. I don't know what I ever did to deserve you."

She pulled back and smiled at him, dashing her hand over her eyes. "You didn't do anything special except make me fall in love with you."

"Oh, Chloe," his voice broke. "I love you, too." He brushed her hair back from her face and kissed her softly. She kissed him back with all the love bursting from her chest.

It was a good minute later before she lightly pulled back, though she kept her hands around his neck. "I'll move. It's no big deal."

He shook his head. "No."

"No?"

"I don't want you to live in Newberg. I'd wanted . . . well, I'd hoped I could bring myself to accept you being here, that I could learn to like being here myself. But," his gaze was adorably pleading, "and please don't stop loving me, I don't think I can do it. I'm glad I came in and got these," he glanced at his poems, "but I'm ready to move on. I'd like to sell the house."

She had no problem with any of that. Except . . . "Okay, but where am I supposed to live if I don't take the place in Newberg?"

He gave her a crooked smile that held a hint of uncertainty that was so endearing, she wanted to kiss him senseless. "With me, of course. If you don't mind the bachelor loft. We can find something else, if you like."

She grinned. "The bachelor loft is fine with me, but aren't you afraid we're rushing things? We've only known each other, what, a week and a half?"

He traced his finger along the side of her face and gazed into her eyes. "I'm afraid of a lot of things, but not of my feelings for you or of our future together. Yes, it's quick, but I've spent so long in the dark, I'm desperate for the light. And you're my light, Chloe. My love."

Tears threatened again, but these came from joy and love and happiness. "I love you, Derek."

"Do you still need help with the popcorn strings?" he asked.

"Sure, but," she was confused, "aren't we going to leave?"

"Tomorrow, I think. I'd like to decorate your tree and maybe have dinner. I'd like my last memory of this house to be the best one."

Love spilled from Chloe's heart and warmed every inch of her. She kissed him again. "Welcome home, Derek."

Epilogue

Rain battered the wide windows in the Archers' kitchen as Derek walked in to refill his and Chloe's pint glasses. Rob was checking the ham in the oven for Christmas Eve dinner and turned when he heard Derek come in.

"You like that?" Rob asked, gesturing to the tap where he'd just hooked up his latest creation that morning. A dark amber with a little spice, it was unusual in its taste, but very usual in its excellence.

"It's great," Derek said. "So great that I think it might get Chloe drunk."

Rob laughed. "Oops. She's a smart girl. She'll keep her head about her."

"If she's so smart, what in the world is she doing with me?" Derek asked, still amazed that she'd welcomed him back after he'd continuously behaved like an utter jackass.

"Improving you. Just let it happen, son." Rob came over and clapped him on the back. "Emily's been doing it for thirty-five years, and I have no complaints."

"Oh, I definitely have no complaints and freely admit she's the best thing that's ever happened to me." He finished drawing the second pint and gave Rob a serious look. "But your family is a very close second."

"And I'll take that ranking." Rob beamed. He'd been overjoyed when Derek had announced that Chloe was moving in with him.

They walked back into the living room together where Chloe, Emily, Alex, Sara, and Hayden were chatting over their various drinks and a spread of hors d'oeuvres that could easily take the place of dinner. The rest of the Archer kids weren't coming home for the holiday, but that made Derek less irritated than usual, with the exception of Kyle. He was overdue for a visit home, and if Derek had understood the importance of family before, its significance had only grown since he'd fallen in love with Chloe. Kyle didn't know what he was missing.

Derek walked to where Chloe was sitting in a stuffed chair and reached down to massage her shoulder. She was laughing at something Hayden had said. Derek leaned down, "Care to steal a moment alone with me?"

She turned her head and looked up at him, her hazel eyes sparkling in the warm glow from the Christmas tree and the roaring fire burning in the hearth. "Definitely."

"Excuse us for a sec." Derek helped her to stand,

handed her the pint glass, and led her from the living room. He took her downstairs to the billiards room.

"You wanted to play pool?" she asked.

"No. I wanted to thank you for introducing me to your parents this morning. I see what you mean about your mom." Even over Skype, Derek could tell Barbara English was uptight. She'd commented multiple times on Chloe's appearance—positively, but still critically—and had then grilled Derek about his background. That he was a CFO of a successful corporation had scored him major points, as had the backdrop of the call—his well-appointed loft.

The Englishes had been tentative in their congratulations upon hearing that Chloe and Derek were living together, but Derek had soothed their fears when he'd secretly called them back a couple of hours ago and shared his master plan.

"I brought you down here to ask you something very important." He bit his tongue to keep from laughing. He'd planned this down to the last detail.

She set her beer on the edge of the pool table. Her eyes widened and he could see the wheels turning in her mind. It was Christmas Eve, they were head over heels in love, and he'd brought her somewhere private to ask a question. There was only one thing going through her mind—just the way he wanted it. "You did?"

He nodded. "Uh-huh. Turns out Uncle Ted wants to retire, and Rob wants you to be Archer Pubs' new artist."

"What?" The tone of her question was equal parts

happy surprise and unexpected shock. While she liked the question, it wasn't the one she'd expected.

Derek stifled his smile. "The hours will be flexible, so you can still teach at the school. Granted, you'll have to travel a bit to paint the actual spaces, but I'll come along, if you like."

She stared at him. "Oh. Um, sure." She shook her head and Derek almost felt sorry for her. Almost. "I'd love to. I mean, thank you, I'm thrilled." She smiled and he knew she really was thrilled beneath her bewilderment.

"So about that pool game . . ." He walked over to the wall and picked up a cue. "Why don't you get the balls?"

She continued to stare at him. Then her brow wrinkled and she pursed her lips. "You want to play pool? Now?"

"Sure, why not?" he asked, inflecting as much inno-cence into his tone as he could.

"Okay . . . I guess. Why didn't you invite the others to come with us?" She fished three balls out of the center pocket on her side. Then she moved to the corner and Derek held his breath. She reached into the pocket and frowned. When her hand came out, she was clutching a box. Derek still managed to keep himself from grinning like an idiot.

"Derek, what is this?" She looked at the box in her palm and then raised her gaze to his.

He moved around the pool table and kneeled in front of her as she opened the lid. The 1.2-carat oval diamond he'd bought in Portland three days ago winked up at her as she gasped.

"Derek!"

"Isn't that what you were expecting when I brought you down here?" He let the smile into his voice and onto his face. "I never, ever want to disappoint you again."

She lifted her gaze from the diamond and looked at him, tears swimming in her magnificent eyes. "It's beautiful."

He reached up and took the ring, then set the box on the edge of the pool table. "Chloe, you've changed my life in more ways than I ever could have hoped. You've given me friendship, support, love, and most of all—a home. I've never felt that so completely before, not even here, but with you, I feel that anything is possible. That *everything* is possible. Will you be my wife?"

She wiped a tear from her cheek. "My mother is going to freak."

"Your mother approves."

She gaped at him. "You asked her?"

"And your dad, of course. They were much more at ease with our living arrangements knowing that we were going to be engaged."

She gave him a skeptical look that he knew was patently false. "You were that sure of my answer, huh?"

"I was . . . hopeful." Something he'd never been before. "But don't leave me hanging. You accepted the job faster than you're accepting me."

"Yes, yes, a million times yes!" She grinned.

He took her left hand and pushed the ring onto her finger. She tugged him to stand and threw her arms around his neck. After a short, but heated kiss, she pulled back. "Do the Archers know?"

"Not yet." He'd wanted to savor the surprise of telling them in person—with Chloe. "I wanted all of my family together when I told them."

"Then let's go do it," she said, clasping his hand.

He let her lead the way, but stopped at the base of the stairs and drew her back for another kiss. "I love you, Chloe. Thank you."

"For what? Loving you? Couldn't help it, I'm afraid."

"But you know what I mean, right? That you're my family? My home?"

She moved to the bottom step of the stairs so she could look him squarely in the eye and cradled his face in her hands. "We're both home now."

Want more Archers and Ribbon Ridge? Grab *Get Lucky*, featuring Sara Archer:

After a hot one-night stand with her old high school crush, Sara isn't sure she wants to hire him to oversee the renovation project she and her siblings are undertaking. But she's outvoted, and now she and Dylan must fight their sizzling mutual attraction or agree to be friends with benefits. When their secret affair starts to become something more, they will have to overcome family drama and emotional trauma to pursue a love that was only in their dreams.

Ribbon Ridge is a fictional town based on several cities and towns dotting the Willamette Valley between Portland and the Oregon Coast. It's pinot noir wine country, very beautiful and picturesque, and a short drive from where I live. My brother actually dwells right in the heart of it in a tiny town with no stoplights. There is, however, an amazing antique mall in an historic schoolhouse (and apparently seven Pokestops).

Would you like to know when my next book is available and to hear about sales and deals? **Sign up for my VIP newsletter** which is the only place you can get bonus books and material such as the short prequel to the Phoenix Club series, INVITATION, and the exciting prequel to Legendary Rogues, THE LEGEND OF A ROGUE.

Join me on social media!

Facebook: https://facebook.com/DarcyBurkeFans
Facebook group: Darcy's Duchesses
Instagram at darcyburkeauthor
Pinterest at darcyburkewrite

And follow me on Bookbub to receive updates on pre-orders, new releases, and deals!

I hope you'll consider leaving a review at your favorite online vendor or networking site!

I appreciate my readers so much. Thank you, thank you, *thank you*.

Acknowledgments

Special thank you to Holly vanSchaick, a Washington firefighter who was incredibly kind to answer all of my questions about how to put out a fire. Holly actually saved two kittens who were temporarily blind and consequently trying to get *into* a burning building for warmth. Thank you for being a hero, Holly; your service is awesome and incredibly appreciated. (And thank you Rachel Grant for putting us together AND for reading. You rock, as usual.)

Also by Darcy Burke

Contemporary Romance

Ribbon Ridge

Let Go (a prequel novella)

Get Lucky

Sparks Fly

Fall Hard

Can't Stop

Break Free

Hold Me

Turn On

So Right

This Love

Historical Mystery

Raven & Wren

A Whisper of Death

A Whisper at Midnight

A Whisper and a Curse

A Whisper in the Shadows

A Whisper of Secrecy

A Whisper in Darkness

Historical Romance

Rogue Rules

If the Duke Dares

Because the Baron Broods

When the Viscount Seduces

As the Earl Likes

Until the Rake Surrenders

Since the Marquess Demands

What the Scoundrel Desires

How the Devil Sins

The Phoenix Club

Improper

Impassioned

Intolerable

Indecent

Impossible

Irresistible

Impeccable

Insatiable

Marrywell Brides

Beguiling the Duke

Romancing the Heiress

Matching the Marquess

The Matchmaking Chronicles

Yule Be My Duke

The Rigid Duke

The Bachelor Earl (also prequel to *The Untouchables*)

The Runaway Viscount

The Make-Believe Widow

The Untouchables

The Bachelor Earl (prequel)

The Forbidden Duke

The Duke of Daring

The Duke of Deception

The Duke of Desire

The Duke of Defiance

The Duke of Danger

The Duke of Ice

The Duke of Ruin

The Duke of Lies

The Duke of Seduction

The Duke of Kisses

The Duke of Distraction

The Untouchables: The Spitfire Society

Never Have I Ever with a Duke

A Duke is Never Enough

A Duke Will Never Do

The Untouchables: The Pretenders

A Secret Surrender

A Scandalous Bargain

A Rogue to Ruin

Love is All Around

(*A Regency Holiday Trilogy*)

The Red Hot Earl

The Gift of the Marquess

Joy to the Duke

Wicked Dukes Club

One Night for Seduction by Erica Ridley

One Night of Surrender by Darcy Burke

One Night of Passion by Erica Ridley

One Night of Scandal by Darcy Burke

One Night to Remember by Erica Ridley

One Night of Temptation by Darcy Burke

Secrets and Scandals

Her Wicked Ways

His Wicked Heart

To Seduce a Scoundrel

To Love a Thief (a novella)

Never Love a Scoundrel

Scoundrel Ever After

Legendary Rogues

Lady of Desire

Romancing the Earl

Lord of Fortune

Captivating the Scoundrel

About the Author

Darcy Burke is the USA Today Bestselling Author of sexy, emotional historical and contemporary romance. Darcy wrote her first book at age 11, a happily ever after about a swan addicted to magic and the female swan who loved him, with exceedingly poor illustrations. Join her Reader Club newsletter for the latest updates from Darcy.

A native Oregonian, Darcy lives on the edge of wine country with her guitar-strumming husband, incredibly talented artist daughter, and imaginative, Japanese-speaking son who will almost certainly out-write her one day (that may be tomorrow). They're a crazy cat family with two Bengal cats, a small, fame-seeking cat named after a fruit, an older rescue Maine Coon with attitude to spare, an adorable former stray who wandered onto their deck and into their hearts, and two bonded boys who used to belong to (separate) neighbors but chose them instead. You can find Darcy in her comfy writing chair balancing her laptop and a cat or three, attempting yoga, folding laundry (which she loves), or wildlife spotting and playing games with her family. She loves traveling to the UK and visiting her beloved cousins in Denmark. Visit Darcy online at www.darcyburke.com and follow her on social media.

facebook.com/DarcyBurkeFans

instagram.com/darcyburkeauthor

pinterest.com/darcyburkewrites

goodreads.com/darcyburke

bookbub.com/authors/darcy-burke

amazon.com/author/darcyburke

threads.net/@darcyburkeauthor

tiktok.com/@darcyburkeauthor